THE LEGION OF LAZARUS

By
EDMOND HAMILTON

ARMCHAIR FICTION
PO Box 4369, Medford, Oregon 97504

A DEATH SENTENCE IN OUTER SPACE!

Death by execution out in the realms of outer space was a pretty horrendous affair. It wasn't like the good old days of the past when they tied you securely into a metal chair, blindfolded you, and dropped a lethal gas pellet into a bucket of cool water sitting just in front of you; or like the nostalgic days when they used to throw a switch and send a sizzling charge of electricity searing through the entire length of your body, leaving you a smoldering pile of dead flesh. No—this was the future. And being expelled from an air lock into deep space was now the legal method of execution!

But being put through this ordeal was also the only way a man could qualify for…The Legion Of Lazarus.

FOR A COMPLETE SECOND NOVEL, TURN TO PAGE 87

ABOUT EDMOND HAMILTON

Edmond Hamilton...

...started writing science fiction when he was 20 years old—all the way back in 1924. Many of his first sci-fi stories were published in *Weird Tales,* but he wrote for all the major pulp and digest magazines for the next several decades. In his career he wrote hundreds of stories and dozens of novels.

Hamilton was born in Ohio in 1904 but lived for many years in Pennsylvania. One of his oldest friends was another master sci-fi storyteller, Jack Williamson.

In 1946, Hamilton married fellow sci-fi writer and enthusiast, Leigh Brackett. They lived for many years in a 130-year old farmhouse in the old Western Reserve of Ohio.

Edmond Hamilton is known as one of the great sci-fi authors of the 20th Century. He passed away in 1977. Some of his best known works were *The Star Kings, City at World's End,* and *The Haunted Stars.*

FOREWORD

It isn't the dying itself. It's what comes before. The waiting, alone in a room without windows, trying to think. The opening of the door, the voices of the men who are going with you but not all the way, the walk down the corridor to the airlock room, the faces of the men, closed and impersonal. They do not enjoy this. Neither do they shrink from it. It's their job.

This is the room. It is small and it has a window. Outside there is no friendly sky, no clouds. There is space, and there is the huge red circle of Mars filling the sky, looking down like an enormous eye upon this tiny moon. But you do not look up. You look out.

There are men out there. They are quite naked. They sleep upon the barren plain, drowsing in a timeless ocean. Their bodies are white as ivory and their hair is loose across their faces. Some of them seem to smile. They lie, and sleep, and the great red eye looks at them forever as they are borne around it.

"It isn't so bad," says one of the men who are with you inside this ultimate room. "Fifty years from now, the rest of us will all be old, or dead."

It is small comfort.

The one garment you have worn is taken from you and the lock door opens, and the fear that cannot possibly become greater does become greater, and then suddenly that terrible crescendo is past. There is no longer any hope, and you learn that without hope there is little to be afraid of. You want now only to get it over with.

You step forward into the lock.

The door behind you shuts. You sense that the one before you is opening, but there is not much time. The burst of air carries you forward. Perhaps you scream, but you are now beyond sound, beyond sight, beyond everything. You do not even feel that it is cold.

5

CHAPTER ONE

There is a time for sleep, and a time for waking. But Hyrst had slept heavily, and the waking was hard. He had slept long, and the waking was slow. *Fifty years*, said the dim voice of remembrance. But another part of his mind said, No, it is only tomorrow morning.

Another part of his mind. That was strange. There seemed to be more parts to his mind than he remembered having had before, but they were all confused and hidden behind a veil of mist. Perhaps they were not really there at all. Perhaps—

Fifty years. I have been dead, he thought, *and now I live again. Half a century. Strange.*

Hyrst lay on a narrow bed, in a place of subdued light and antiseptic-smelling air. There was no one else in the room. There was no sound.

Fifty years, he thought. *What is it like now, the house where I lived once, the country, the planet? Where are my children, where are my friends, my enemies, the people I loved, the people I hated?*

Where is Elena? Where is my wife?

A whisper out of nowhere, sad, remote. *Your wife is dead and your children are old. Forget them. Forget the friends and the enemies.*

But I can't forget! cried Hyrst silently in the spaces of his own mind. It was only yesterday—

Fifty years, said the whisper. *And you must forget.*

MacDonald, said Hyrst suddenly. *I didn't kill him. I was innocent. I can't forget that.*

Careful, said the whisper. *Watch out.*

I didn't kill MacDonald. Somebody did. Somebody let me pay for it. Who? Was it Landers? Was it Saul? We four were together out there on Titan, when he died.

Careful, Hyrst. *They're coming. Listen to me. You think this is your own mind speaking, question-and-answer. But it isn't.*

Hyrst sprang upright on the narrow bed, his heart pounding, the sweat running cold on his skin. *Who are you? Where are you? How—*

They're here, said the whisper calmly. *Be quiet.*

Two men came into the ward. "I am Dr. Merridew," said the one in the white coverall, smiling at Hyrst with a brisk professional smile. "This is Warden Meister. We didn't mean to startle you. There are a few questions, before we release you—"

Merridew, said the whisper in Hyrst's mind, *is a psychiatrist. Let me handle this.*

Hyrst sat still, his hands lax between his knees, his eyes wide and fixed in astonishment. He heard the psychiatrist's questions, and he heard the answers he gave to them, but he was merely an instrument, with no conscious volition, it was the whisperer in his mind who was answering. Then the warden shuffled some papers he held in his hand and asked questions of his own.

"You underwent the Humane Penalty without admitting your guilt. For the record, now that the penalty has been paid, do you wish to change your final statements?"

The voice in Hyrst's mind, the secret voice, said swiftly to him. *Don't argue with them, don't get angry, or they'll keep you on and on here.*

"But—" thought Hyrst.

I know you're innocent, but they'll never believe it. They'll keep you on for further psychiatric tests. They might get near the truth, Hyrst—the truth about us.

Suddenly Hyrst began to understand, not all and not clearly, something of what had happened to him. The obscuring mists began to lift from the borders of his mind.

"What is the truth," he asked in that inner quiet, "about us?"

Being expelled from an air lock into deep space was the legal method of execution. But it was also the only way a man could qualify for—

The Legion Of Lazarus

by

Edmond Hamilton

IT ISN'T the dying itself. It's what comes before. The waiting, alone in a room without windows, trying to think. The opening of the door, the voices of the men who are going with you but not all the way, the walk down the corridor to the airlock room, the faces of the men, closed and impersonal. They do not enjoy this. Neither do they shrink from it. It's their job.

You've spent fifty years in the Valley of the Shadow. You're changed, Hyrst. You're not quite human any more. No one is who goes through the freeze. But they don't know that.

"Then you too—"

Yes. And I too changed. And that is why our minds can speak, even though I am on Mars and you are on its moon. But they must not know that. So don't argue, don't show emotion!

The warden was waiting. Hyrst said aloud to him, slowly. "I have no statement to make."

The warden did not seem surprised. He went on, "According to your papers here you also denied knowing the location of the Titanite for which MacDonald was presumably murdered. Do you still deny that?"

Hyrst was honestly surprised. "But surely, by now—"

The warden shrugged. "According to this data, it never came to light."

"I never knew," said Hyrst, "where it was."

"Well," said the warden, "I've asked the question and that's as far as my responsibility goes. But there's a visitor who has permission to see you."

HE AND the doctor went out. Hyrst watched them go. He thought, *So I'm not quite human. Not quite human any more. Does that make me more, or less, than a man?*

Both, said the secret voice. *Their minds are still closed to you. Only our minds—we who have changed too—are open.*

"Who are you?" asked Hyrst.

My name is Shearing. Now listen. When you are released, they'll bring you down here to Mars. I'll be waiting for you. I'll help you.

"Why? What do you care about me, or a murder fifty years old?"

I'll tell you why later, said the whisper of Shearing. *But you must follow my guidance. There's danger for you, Hyrst, from the moment you're released! There are those who have been waiting for you.*

"Danger? But—"

The door opened, and Hyrst's visitor came in. He was a man something over sixty but the deep lines in his face made him look older. His face was gray and drawn and twitching, but it became perfectly rigid and white when he came to the foot of the bed and looked at Hyrst. There was rage in his eyes, a rage so old and weary that it brought tears to them.

"You should have stayed dead," he said to Hyrst. "Why couldn't they let you stay dead?"

Hyrst was shocked and startled. "Who are you? And why—"

The other man was not even listening. His eyelids had closed, and when they opened again they looked on naked agony. "It isn't right," he said. "A murderer should die, and stay dead. Not come back."

"I didn't murder MacDonald," Hyrst said, with the beginnings of anger. "And I don't know why you—"

He stopped. The white, aging face, the tear-filled, furious eyes, he did not quite know what there was about them but it was there, like an old remembered face peeping up through a blur of water for a moment, and then withdrawing again.

After a moment, Hyrst said hoarsely, "What's your name?"

"You wouldn't know it," said the other. "I changed it, long ago."

Hyrst felt a cold, and it seemed that he could not breathe. He said, "But you were only eleven—"

He could not go on. There was a terrible silence between them. He must break it, he could not let it go on. He must speak. But all he could say was to whisper, "I'm not a murderer. You must believe it. I'm going to prove it—"

11

"You murdered MacDonald. And you murdered my mother. I watched her age and die, spending every penny, spending every drop of her blood and ours, to get you back again. I pretended for fifty years that I too believed you were innocent, when all the time I knew."

Hyrst said, "I'm innocent." He tried to say a name, too, but he could not speak the word.

"No. You're lying, as you lied then. We found out. Mother hired detectives, experts. Over and over, for decades—and always they found the same thing. Landers and Saul could not possibly have killed MacDonald, and you were the only other human being there. Proof? I can show you barrels of it. And all of it proof that my father was a murderer."

He leaned a little toward Hyrst, and the tears ran down his lined, careworn face. He said, "All right, you've come back. Alive, still young. But I'm warning you. If you try again to get that Titanite, if you shame us all again after all this time, if you even come near us, I'll kill you."

He went out. Hyrst sat, looking after him, and he thought that no man before him had ever felt what tore him now.

Inside his mind came Shearing's whisper, with a totally unexpected note of compassion. *But some of us have, Hyrst. Welcome to the brotherhood. Welcome to the Legion of Lazarus.*

CHAPTER TWO

Mars roared and glittered tonight. And how was a man to stand the faces and lights and sounds, when he had come back from the silence of eternity?

Hyrst walked through the flaring streets of Syrtis City with slow and dragging steps. It was like being back on Earth. For this city was not really part of the old dead planet, of the dark barrens that rolled away beneath the night. This was the place of the rocket-men, the miners, the schemers, the workers, who had come from another, younger world. Their bars and entertainment houses flung a sun-like brilliance. Their ships, lifting majestically skyward from the distant spaceport, wrote their flaming sign on the sky. Only here and there moved one of the hooded, robed humanoids who had once owned this world.

The next corner, said the whisper in Hyrst's mind. *Turn there. No, not toward the spaceport. The other way.*

Hyrst thought suddenly, "Shearing."

Yes?

"I am being followed."

His physical ears heard nothing but the voices and music. His physical eyes saw only the street crowd. Yet he knew. He knew it by a picture that kept coming into his mind, of a blurred shape moving always behind him.

Of course you're being followed, came Shearing's thought. *I told you they've been waiting for you. This is the corner. Turn.*

Hyrst turned. It was a darker street, running away from the lights through black warehouses and on the labyrinthine monolithic houses of the humanoids.

Now look back, Shearing commanded. *No, not with your eyes! With your mind. Learn to use your talents.*

Hyrst tried. The blurred image in his mind came clearer, and clearer still, and it was a young man with a vicious mouth and flat uncaring eyes. Hyrst shivered. "Who is he?"

He works for the men who have been waiting for you, Hyrst. Bring him this way.

"This—way?"

Look ahead. With your mind. Can't you learn?

Stung to sudden anger, Hyrst flung out a mental probe with a power he hadn't known he possessed. In a place of total darkness between two warehouses ahead, he saw a tall man lounging at his ease. Shearing laughed.

Yes, it's me. Just walk past me. Don't hurry.

Hyrst glanced backward, mentally at the man following him through the shadows. He was closer now, and quite silent. His face was tight and secret. Hyrst thought, *How do I know this Shearing isn't in it with him, taking me into a place where they can both get at me—*

He went past the two warehouses and he did not turn his head but his mind saw Shearing waiting in the darkness. Then there was a soft, shapeless sound, and he turned and saw Shearing bending over a huddled form.

"That was unkind of you," said Shearing, speaking aloud but not loudly.

Hyrst, still shaking, said, "But not exactly strange. I've never seen you before. And I still don't know what this is all about."

Shearing smiled, as he knelt beside the prone, unmoving body. Even here in the shadows, Hyrst could see him with these new eyes of the mind. Shearing was a big man. His hair was grizzled along the sides of his head, and his eyes were dark and very keen. He reached out one hand and turned the head of the prone young man, and they looked at the lax, loose face.

"He's not dead?" said Hyrst.

"Of course not. But it will be a while before he wakes."

"But who is he?"

Shearing stood up. "I never saw him before. But I know who he's working for."

HYRST flung a sudden question at Shearing, and almost without thinking he followed it to surprise the answer in Shearing's mind. The question was, *Who are you working for?* And the answer was a woman, a tall and handsome woman with angry eyes, standing against a drift of stars. There was a ship, all lonely on a dark plain, and she was pointing to it, and somehow Hyrst knew that it was vitally important to her, and to Shearing, and perhaps even to himself. But before he could do more than register this fleeting vision on his own consciousness, Shearing's mind slammed shut with exactly the same violent effect as a door slammed in his face. He reeled back, throwing up his arms in a futile but instinctive gesture, and Shearing said angrily,

"You're getting too good. I'll give you a social hint—it's customary to knock before you enter."

Hyrst said, still holding the pieces of his head together, "All right—sorry. So who is she?"

"She's one of us. She wants what we want."

"I want only to find out who murdered MacDonald!"

"You want more than that, Hyrst, though you don't know it yet. But MacDonald's murderer is part of what we're after."

He took Hyrst's arm. "We don't have long. Thanks to my guidance, you slipped them all except this one. But they'll be hounding after our trail very quickly."

They went on along the shadowed street. The glare of the lights died back behind them, and they moved in darkness with only the keen stars to watch them, and the cold, gritty wind blowing in from the barrens, and the dark door-ways of the mastaba-like monolithic houses of the humanoids staring at them like sightless eyes. Hyrst looked up at the bright, tiny moon that crept amid the stars, and a deep shaking took him as he thought of men lying up there in the deathly sleep, of himself lying there year after year....

"In here," said Shearing. It was one of the frigid, musty tombs that the humanoids called home. It was dark and there was nothing in it at all. "We can't risk a light. We don't need it, anyway."

They sat down. Hyrst said desperately, "Listen, I want to know some things. Exactly what are we doing here?"

Shearing answered deliberately, "We are hiding from those who want you, and we are waiting for a chance to go to our friends."

"Our friends? Your friends, maybe. That woman—I don't know her, and—"

"Now *you* listen, Hyrst. I'll tell you this much about us now. We're Lazarites, like you, with the same powers as you. But all Lazarites are not on *our* side."

Hyrst thought about that. "Then those others who are hunting us—"

"There are Lazarites among them, too. Not many, but a few. You don't know us, you don't know them. Do you want to leave me and go back out and let them have you?"

Hyrst remembered the adder-like face of the young man who had come after him through the shadows. After a long moment he said, "Well. But what are *you* after?"

"The thing that MacDonald was killed for, fifty years ago."

Hyrst said, "The Titanite? They said it hadn't ever been found. But how it could have remained hidden so long—"

"I want you," Shearing said, "to tell me all about how MacDonald died. Everything you can remember."

Hyrst asked eagerly, "You think we can find out who killed him? After all this time? God, if we could—my son—"

"Quiet, Hyrst. Go ahead and tell me. Not in words. Just remember what happened, and I'll get it."

Yet, by sheer lifetime habit, Hyrst could not remember without first putting it into words in his own mind, as they two sat in the cold, whispering darkness.

"There were four of us out there on Titan, you must already know that. And only four—"

FOUR MEN. And one was named MacDonald, an engineer, a secretive, selfish and enormously greedy man. MacDonald was the man who found a fortune, and kept it secret, and died.

Landers was one. A lean, brown, lively man, an excellent physicist with a friendly manner and no obvious ambitions.

Saul was one, and he was big and blond and quiet, a good drinking companion, a good geologist, a lover of good music. If he had any darker passions, he kept them hidden.

Hyrst was the fourth man, and the only one of the four still living....

He remembered now. He saw the black and bitter crags of Titan stark against the glory of the Rings, and he saw two figures moving across a plain of methane snow, their helmets gleaming in the Saturn-light. Behind them in the plain were the flat, half-buried concrete structures of the little refinery, and all around them were the spidery roads where the big half-tracs dragged their loads of uranium ore from the enchaining mountains.

The two men were quarrelling.

"You're angry," MacDonald was saying, "because it was *I* who found it."

"Listen," Hyrst said. "We're sick, all three of us, of hearing you brag about it."

"I'll bet you are," said MacDonald smugly. "The first find of a Titanite pocket for years. The rarest, costliest stuff in the System. If you know the way they've been bidding to buy it from me—"

"I do know," Hyrst said. "You've done nothing for weeks but give forth mysterious hints—"

"And you don't like that," MacDonald said. "Of course you don't! It's no part of our refinery deal, it's mine, I've got it and it's hidden where nobody can find it till I sell it. Naturally, you don't like that."

"All *right*," said Hyrst. "So the Titanite find is all yours. You're still a partner in the refinery, remember. And you've still got an obligation to the rest of us, so you can damn well get in and do your job."

"Don't worry. I've always done my job."

"More or less," said Hyrst. "For your information, I've seen better engineers in grade-school. There's Number Three hoist. It's been busted for a week. Now let's get in there and fix it."

The two figures in Hyrst's memory toiled on, out of the area of roads to the edge of the landing field, where the ships come to take away the refined uranium. Number Three hoist rose in a stiff, ugly column from the ground. It was supposed to fetch the uranium up from the underground storage bins and load it into a specially-built hot-tank ship in position at the dock. But Number Three had balked and refused to perform its task. In this completely automated plant, men were only important when something went wrong. Now something was wrong, and it was up to MacDonald, the mechanical engineer, and Hyrst, the electronics man, to set it right.

Hyrst opened the hatch, and they climbed the metal stairs to the upper chamber. Number Three's brain was here, its scanners, its tabulating and recording apparatus, its signal system. A red light pulsated on a panel, alone in a string of white ones.

"Trouble's in the hoist-mechanism," said Hyrst. "That's your department." He smiled and sat down on a metal bench in the center of the room, with his back to the stair. "D Level."

MacDonald grumbled, and went to a skeletal cage built over a round segment of the floor. Various tools were clipped to the ribs of the cage. MacDonald pulled an extra rayproof protectall over his vac-suit and stepped inside the cage, pressing a button. The cage dropped, into a circular shaft that paralleled the hoist right down to the feeder mechanism.

Hyrst waited. Inside his helmet he could hear MacDonald breathing and grumbling as he worked away, repairing a break in the belt. He did not hear anything else. Then something happened, so swiftly that he had never had any memory of it, and some time later he came to and looked for MacDonald. The cage was way down at the bottom of the shaft and MacDonald was in it, with a very massive pedestal-block on top of him. The block had been unbolted from the floor and dragged to the edge of the shaft, and it could not possibly have been an accident that it tumbled in, between the wide-apart ribs of the cage.

And that's how MacDonald died, Hyrst thought—and so *I* died. They said I forced the secret of his Titanite find out of him, and then killed him.

Shearing asked swiftly, "MacDonald never gave you any hint of where he'd hidden the Titanite?"

"No," said Hyrst. He paused, and then said, "It's the Titanite you're after?"

Shearing answered carefully. "In a way, yes. But *we* didn't kill MacDonald for it. Those who did kill him are the men who are after you now. They're afraid you might lead us to the stuff."

Hyrst swore, shaking with sudden anger. "Damn it, I won't be treated like a child. Not by you, by anyone. I want—"

"You want the men who killed MacDonald," said Shearing. "I know. I remember what was in your mind when you met your son."

A weakness took Hyrst and he leaned his forehead against the cold stone wall.

"I'm sorry," said Shearing. "But we want what you want—and more. So much more that you can't dream it. You must trust us."

"Us? That woman?"

ONCE again in Shearing's mind Hyrst saw the woman with her head against the stars, and the ship looming darkly. He saw the woman much more clearly, and she was like a fire, burning with anger, burning with a single-minded, dedicated purpose. She was beautiful, and frightening.

"She, and others," said Shearing. "Listen. We must go soon. We're to be picked up, secretly. Will you trust us—or would you rather trust yourself to those who are hunting you?"

Hyrst was silent. Shearing said, "Well?"

"I'll go with you," said Hyrst.

They went out into the cold darkness, and Hyrst heard Shearing say in his mind, "I wouldn't try to run—"

But it wasn't Shearing speaking in his mind now, it was a third man.

"I wouldn't try to run—"

Frantically startled, Hyrst threw out his mental vision and saw the men who stood around them in the darkness, four men, three of them holding the wicked little weapons called bee-guns in their hands. The fourth man came closer, a dark slender man with a face like a fox, high-boned, narrow-eyed, smiling. It came to Hyrst that the three with weapons were only ordinary men, and that it was this fourth man whose mind had spoken.

He was speaking aloud now. "I want you alive, believe me—but there are endless gradations between alive and dead. My men are very accurate."

Shearing's face was suddenly drawn and exhausted. "Don't try anything," he warned Hyrst wearily. "He means it."

The dark man shook his head at Shearing. "This wasn't nice of you. You knew we had a particular interest in Mr. Hyrst." He turned to Hyrst and smiled. His teeth were small and very neat and white. "Did you know that Shearing has been keeping a shield over your mind as well as his? A little too large a task for him. When you jarred his mind open for an instant, it was all we needed to lead us here."

He went on. "Mr. Hyrst, my name is Vernon. We'd like you to come with us."

Vernon nodded to the three accurate men, and the whole little group began to walk in the direction of the spaceport. Shearing seemed almost asleep on his feet now. It was as though he had expended all his energy on a task, and failed at it, and was now quiescent, like an empty well waiting to fill again.

"Where are we going?" Hyrst asked, and Vernon answered:

"To see a gentleman you've never heard of, in a place you've never been." He added, with easy friendliness, "Don't worry, Mr. Hyrst, we have nothing against *you*. You're new to this—ah—state of life. You shouldn't be asked to make decisions or agreements until you know both sides of the question. Mr. Shearing was taking an unfair advantage."

Remembering the dark hard purpose Shearing had let him see in his mind, Hyrst could not readily dispute that. But he put out an exploring probe in the direction of Vernon's mind.

It was shut tight.

They walked on, toward the spaceport gates.

CHAPTER THREE

All space was before him, hung with the many-colored lights of the stars, intensely brilliant in the black nothing. It was incredibly splendid, but it was too much like what he had looked at with his cold unseeing eyes for fifty years. He looked down—down being relative to where he was standing in the blister-window—and saw the whole Belt swarming by under him like a drift of fireflies. He quivered inwardly with a chill vertigo, and turned away.

Vernon was talking aloud. He had been talking for some time. He was stretched out on a soft, deep lounge, smoking, pretending to sip from a tall glass.

"So you see, Mr. Hyrst, we can help you a lot. It's not easy for a Lazarite—for one of us—to get a job. I know. People have a—well, a *feeling*. Now Mr. Bellaver—"

"Where is Shearing?" asked Hyrst. He came and stood in the center of the room, with the soft lights in his eyes and the soft carpets under his feet. His mind reached out, uneasy and restless, but it seemed to be surrounded by a zone of fog that tangled and confused and deflected it. He could not find Shearing.

"We've been here for hours," he said. "Where is he?"

"Probably talking a deal with Mr. Bellaver. I wouldn't worry. As I was saying, Bellaver Incorporated is interested in men like you. We're the largest builders of spacecraft in the System, and we can afford—"

"I know all about it," said Hyrst impatiently. "Old Quentin Bellaver was busy swallowing up his rivals when I went through the door."

"Then," said Vernon imperturbably, "you should realize how much we can do for you. Electronics is a vital branch—"

Hyrst moved erratically around the room, looking at things and not really seeing them, hearing Vernon's voice but not understanding what it said. He was growing more and more uneasy. It was as though someone was calling to him, urgently, but just out of earshot. He kept straining, with his ears and his mind, and Vernon's voice babbled on, and the barrier was like a wall around his thoughts.

They had been aboard this ship for a long time now, and he had not seen Shearing since they came through the hatch. It was not really a ship, of course. It had no power of its own, depending on powerful tugs to tow it. It was Walter Bellaver's floating pleasure-palace, and the damnedest thing Hyrst had ever seen. Vernon said it could and often did accommodate three or four hundred guests in the utmost luxury. There was nobody aboard it now but Bellaver, Vernon, Hyrst and Shearing, the three very accurate men, and perhaps a dozen others including stewards and the crews of the tugs and Bellaver's yacht. It was named the *Happy Dream*, and it was presently drifting in an excessively lonely orbit high above the ecliptic, between nothing and nowhere.

Vernon had been with him almost constantly. He was getting tired of Vernon. Vernon talked too much.

"Listen," he said. "You can stop selling Bellaver. I'm not looking for a job. Where's Shearing?"

"Oh, forget Shearing," said Vernon, impatient in his turn. "You never heard of him until a few days ago."

"He helped me."

"For reasons of his own."

"What's *your* reason? And Bellaver's?"

"Mr. Bellaver is interested in all social problems. And I'm a Lazarite myself, so naturally I have sympathy for others like me." Vernon sat up, putting his glass aside on a low table. He had drunk hardly any of the contents.

"Shearing," he said, "is a member of a gang who some time ago stole a particular property of Bellaver Incorporated. You're not involved in the quarrel, Mr. Hyrst. I'd advise you, as a friend, to stay not involved."

Hyrst's mind and his ears were stretched and quivering, straining to hear a cry for help just a little too far away.

"What kind of a property?" asked Hyrst.

Vernon shrugged. "The Bellavers have never said what kind, for fairly obvious reasons."

"Something to do with ships?"

"I suppose so. It isn't important to me. Nor to you, Mr. Hyrst."

"Will you pour me a drink?" said Hyrst, pointing to the cellaret close beside Vernon. "Yes, that's fine. How long ago?"

"What?" asked Vernon, measuring whisky into a glass.

"The theft," said Hyrst, and threw his mind suddenly against the barrier. For one fleeting second he forced a crack in it. "Something over fifty—", said Vernon, and let the glass fall. He spun around from the cellaret and was halfway to his feet when Hyrst hit him. He hit him three or four times before he would stay down, and three or four more before he would lie quiet. Hyrst straightened up, breathing hard. His lip was bleeding and he wiped it with the back of his hand. "That was a little too big a job for *you*, Mr. Vernon," he said viciously. "Trying to keep my mind blanked and under control for hours." He stuffed a handkerchief into Vernon's mouth, and tied him up with his own cummerbund, and shoved him out of sight behind an enormous bed. Then he opened the door carefully, and went out.

THERE was nobody in the corridor. This was wide and ornate, with doors opening off it, and nothing to show what was behind them or which way to go. Hyrst stood still a minute, getting control of himself. The barrier no longer obscured his mind. He let it rove, finding that every time he did that it was easier, and the images clearer. He heard Shearing again, as he had heard him in that one second when Vernon's guard had faltered. His face became set and ugly. He began to move toward the stern of the *Happy Dream.*

Heavy metal-cloth curtains closed this end of the corridor. Beyond them was a ballroom in which only one dim light now burned, a vastness of black polished floors and crystal windows looking upon space. Hyrst's footsteps were hushed and swallowed up in whispering echoes. He made his way across to another set of curtains, edged between them with infinite caution, and found himself in the upper aisle of an amphitheater.

It was pitch dark where he was, and he stood perfectly still, exploring with his mind. He could not see any guards. The rows of empty seats were arranged in circles around a central pit, large enough for any entertainment Mr. Bellaver might decide to give. The pit was brilliantly lighted, and from somewhere lower down came the intermittent sound of voices.

Also from the pit came Shearing's cries. Hyrst began to tremble with outrage and anger, and his still-uncertain mental control faltered dangerously. Then from out of nowhere, a voice spoke in his mind, and he saw the face of the woman he had seen twice before, the woman Shearing served.

"Careful," she said. "There is a Lazarite with Bellaver. His attention is all on Shearing, but you must keep your mind shielded. I'll help you."

Hyrst whispered. "Thanks." He felt calm now, alert and capable. He crept along the dark aisle, toward the pit.

Mr. Bellaver's theater lacked nothing. The large circular stage area was fitted with upper and lower electro-magnets for the use of acrobats and dancers with null-grav specialties. They could perform without disturbing the regular grav-field of the *Happy Dream*, thus keeping the guests comfortable, and by skillful manipulation of the magnetic fields more spectacular stunts were possible than in ordinary no-gravity.

Shearing was in the pit, between the upper and lower magnets. He wore an acrobat's metal attraction-harness, strapped on over his clothes. When Hyrst looked over the rail he was hanging at the central point of weightlessness, where everything in a man floats free and his senses are lost in a dreadful vertigo unless he has been conditioned over a long period of time to get used to it. Shearing had not been conditioned.

"Careful," said the woman's warning voice in his mind. "His life depends on you. No, don't try to make contact with him! The Lazarite would sense you—"

Shearing began a slow ascension toward the upper magnet as the current was increased, from some unseen control board. He moved convulsively turning horizontally around the axis of his own middle like a toy spun on a string. His back was uppermost, and Hyrst could not see his face.

"Bellaver and the Lazarite," said the woman quietly, "are trying to learn from Shearing where our ship is. He has been able so far to keep his mind shielded. He is—a very brave man. But you'll have to hurry. He's near the breaking point."

Shearing was now almost level with Hyrst, suspended over that open pit, looking down, a long way.

"You'll have to be quick, Hyrst. Please. Please get him out of there before we have to kill him."

The current in the magnet was cut and Shearing fell, with a long neighing scream.

HYRST looked down. The repelling force of the lower magnet cushioned the fall, and the upper magnet took hold, hard. Shearing stopped about three feet above the stage floor and started slowly to rise again. He seemed to be crying. Hyrst turned and ran back to the top of the aisle. Halfway around the circle he found steps and went tearing down them. On the next level—there were three—he saw two men leaning over the broad rail, watching Shearing.

"Yes, there they are. You must find a weapon—"

Hyrst looked around, blinking like a mole in the dark. Seats, nothing but seats. Ornamentation, but all solid. Small metal cylinder, set in a wall niche. Chemical extinguisher. Yes. Compact and heavy. He took it.

"Hurry. He's almost through—"

The two men were tense and hungry, eager as wolves. One was the Lazarite, a grey man, old and seamed with living and none of it good. The other was Bellaver, and he was young. He was tall and fresh-faced, impeccably shaven, impeccably dressed, the keen, clean, public-spirited executive.

"I can give you more if you want it, Shearing," Bellaver said, his fingers ready on a control-plate set into the broad rail. "How about it?"

"Shut up, Bellaver," whispered the Lazarite aloud. "I've almost got it. Almost—" His face was agonized with concentration.

"*Now!*"

The woman's voiceless cry in his mind sent Hyrst forward. His hand swung up and then down in a crashing arc, elongated by the heavy cylinder. The Lazarite fell without a sound. He fell across Bellaver, pushing him back from the control-plate, and lay over his feet, bleeding gently into the thick pile of the carpet. Bellaver's mouth and eyes opened wide. He looked at the Lazarite and then at Hyrst. He leaped backward, away from the encumbrance at his ankles, making the first hoarse effort at a shout for help. Hyrst did not give him time to finish it. The first row of seats caught Bellaver and threw him, and Hyrst swung the cylinder again. Bellaver collapsed.

"Was I in time?" Hyrst asked of the woman, in his mind. He thought she was crying when she answered, "Yes." He smiled. He stepped over the Lazarite and went to the control-plate and began to work with it until he had Shearing safely on the floor of the stage. Then he cut the power and ran down another flight of steps to the bottom level. His mind was able to range free now. He could not sense anyone close at hand. Bellaver seemed to have sent underlings elsewhere in the *Happy Dream* while he worked on Shearing. It was nothing for which a man would seek witnesses. Hyrst vaulted the rail onto the stage and dragged Shearing away from the magnet. He felt uncomfortable in all that glare of light. He hauled and grunted until he got

Shearing over the rail into the dark. Then he wrestled the harness off him. Shearing sobbed feebly, and retched.

"Can you stand up?" said Hyrst. "Hey. Shearing." He shook him, hard. "Stand up."

He got Shearing up, a one-hundred-and-ninety pound rag doll draped over his shoulders. He began to walk him out of the theater. "Are you still there?" he asked of the woman.

The answer came into his mind swiftly. "Yes. I'll help you watch. Do you see where the skiff is?"

It was in a pod under the belly of the *Happy Dream*. "I see it," said Hyrst.

"Take that. Bellaver's yacht is faster, but you'd need the crew. The skiff you can handle yourself."

HE WALKED Shearing into a fore-and-aft corridor. Shearing's feet were beginning to move of their own accord, and he had stopped retching. But his eyes were still blank and he staggered aimlessly. Hyrst's nerves were prickling with a mixture of fierce satisfaction and fear. Far above in the lush suite he felt Vernon stir and come to. There were men somewhere closer, quite close. He forced his mind to see. Two of the very accurate men who had been with Vernon were playing cards with two others who were apparently stewards. The third one lolled in a chair, smoking. All five were in a lounge just around the corner of a transverse corridor. The door was open.

Without realizing that he had done so, Hyrst took control of Shearing's mind. "Steady, now. We're going past that corner without a sound. You hear me, Shearing? Not a sound."

Shearing's eyes flickered vaguely. He frowned, and his step became steadier. The floor of the corridor was covered in a tough resilient plastic that deadened footsteps. They passed the corner. The men continued to play cards. Hyrst sent up a derisive insult to Vernon and told Shearing to hurry a little. The stair leading down into the pod was just ahead, ten yards, five—

A man appeared in the corridor ahead, coming from some storeroom with a rack of plastic bottles in his hand.

"You'll have to run now," came the woman's thought, coolly. "Don't panic. You can still make it."

The man with the bottles yelled. He began to run toward Hyrst and Shearing, dropping the rack to leave his hands free. In the lounge room behind them the card-party broke up. Hyrst took Shearing by the arm and clamped down even tighter on his mind, giving him a single command. They ran together, fast.

The men from the lounge poured out into the main corridor. Their voices were confused and very loud. Ahead, the man who had been bringing the bottles was now between Hyrst and the stair. He was a brown, hard man who looked like a pilot. He said, "You better stop," and then he grappled with Hyrst and Shearing. The three of them spun around in a clumsy dance, Shearing moving like an automaton. Hyrst and the pilot flailing away with their fists, and then the pilot fell back hard on the seat of his pants, with the blood bursting out of his nose and his eyes glazing. Hyrst raced for the stair, propelling Shearing. They tumbled down it with a shot from a bee-gun buzzing over their heads. It was a short stair with a double-hatch door at the bottom. They fell through it, and Hyrst slammed it shut almost on the toes of a man coming down the stair behind them. The automatic lock took hold. Hyrst told Shearing, "You can stop now."

A few minutes later, from the great swag belly of the *Happy Dream*, a small space-skiff shot away and was quickly lost in the star-shot immensity above the Belt.

CHAPTER FOUR

It did not stay lost for long. Shearing was at the controls. The chronometer showed fourteen hours and twenty-seven minutes since they left the *Happy Dream*. Shearing had spent eight of those hours in a species of comatose slumber, from which he had roused out practically normal. Now Hyrst was heavily asleep in the pneumo-chair beside him.

Shearing punched him. "Wake up."

After several more punches Hyrst groaned and opened his eyes. He mumbled a question, and Shearing pointed out the wide curved port that gave full vision forward and on both sides.

"It was a good try," he said, "but I don't think we're going to make it. Look there. No, farther back. See it? Now the other side. And there's one astern."

Still sleepy, but alarmed, Hyrst swung his mental vision around. It was easier than looking. Two fast, powerful tugs from the *Happy Dream*, and Bellaver's yacht. He frowned in heavy concentration. "Bellaver's aboard. He's got a mighty goose-egg on his head. Vernon too, with his shields up tight. The three accurate men and the pilot—his nose is a thing of beauty—plus crew. Nine in all. Two men each to the tugs. The other Lazarite, the one I laid out—he's not along."

Shearing nodded approvingly. "You're getting good. Now take a glance at our fuel-tanks and tell me what you see."

Hyrst sat up straight, fully awake. "Practically," he said, "nothing."

"This skiff was really meant for short hops only. We've probably got enough for perhaps another forty-five minutes, less if we get too involved. They're faster than we are, so they'll catch up to us—oh, say in about half an hour. We have friends coming—"

"Friends?"

"Certainly. You don't think we let each other down, do you? Not the brotherhood. But they had to come from a long way off. We can't possibly rendezvous under an hour and a half, maybe more if—"

"I know," said Hyrst. "If we all get involved." He looked out the port. In the beginning, following directions from the young woman—whose name he had never thought to ask—he had set a course that plunged him deep into one of the wildest sectors of the Belt. He was not a pilot. He could, like most men of his time, handle a simple craft under simple conditions, but these conditions were not simple. The skiff's radar was short-range and it had no automatic deflection reflexes. Hyrst had had to fly on ESP, spotting meteor swarms, asteroids, debris of all sorts in this poetically named hell-hole, the Path of Minor Worlds, and then figuring out how to get by, through, or over them without a crash. Shearing had relieved him just in time.

He glowered at the whirling, glittering mess outside, the dust, the shards and fragments of a shattered world. It merged into mist and his mind was roving again. Shearing jockeyed the controls. He was flying esper too. The tugs and Bellaver's fast yacht were closing up the gap. The level in the tanks went down, used up not in free fall but in the constant maneuvering.

Hyrst swung mentally inboard to check vac-suits and equipment in the locker, and then out again. His vision was strong and free. He could look at the Sun, and see the splendid fires of the corona. He could look at Mars, old and cold and dried-up, and at Jupiter, massive and sullen and totally useless except as an anchor for its family of crazy moons. He could look farther than that. He could look at the stars. In a little while, he thought, he could look at whole galaxies. His heart pounded and the breath came hot and hard into his lungs. It was a good feeling. It made all that had gone before almost worthwhile. The primal immensities drew him, the black gulfs lit with gold and crimson and peacock-colored flames. He wanted to go farther and farther, into—

"You're learning too fast," said Shearing dryly. "Stick to something small and close and sordid, namely an asteroid where we can land."

"I found one," said Hyrst. "There."

Shearing followed his mental nudge. "Hell," he said, "couldn't you have spotted something better? These Valhallas give me the creeps."

"The others within reach are too small, or there's no cover. We'll have quite a little time to wait. I take it you would like to be alive when your friends come."

Vernon's thought broke in on them abruptly. "You have just one chance of that, and that's to give yourselves up, right now."

"Does the socially-conscious Mr. Bellaver still want to give me that job?" asked Hyrst.

"I'm warning you," said Vernon.

"Your mind is full of hate," said Hyrst. "Cleanse it." He shut Vernon out as easily as hanging up a phone. Under stress, his new powers were developing rapidly. He felt a little drunk with them. Shearing said, "Don't get above yourself, boy. You're still a cub, you know." Then he grinned briefly and added, "By the way, thanks."

Hyrst said, "I owed it to you. And you can thank your lady friend, too. She had a big hand in it."

"Christina," said Shearing softly. "Yes."

He dropped the skiff sharply in a descending curve, toward the asteroid.

"Do you think," said Hyrst, "you could now tell me what the devil this is all about?"

Shearing said, "We've got a starship."

Hyrst stared. For a long time he didn't say anything. Then, "You've got a starship? But nobody has! People talk of someday reaching other stars, but nobody tried yet, nobody *could* try—" He broke off, suddenly remembering a dark, lonely ship, and a woman with angry eyes watching it. Even in his astonishment, things began to come clearer to him. "So that's it—a starship. And Bellaver wants it?"

Shearing nodded.

"Well," said Hyrst. "Go on."

"You've already developed some amazing mental capabilities since you came back from beyond the door. You'll find that's only the beginning. The radiation, the exposure—something. The simple act of pseudo-death, perhaps. Anyway, the brain is altered, stepped up, a great deal of its normally unused potential released. You've always been a fair-to-middling technician. You'll find your rating boosted, eventually, to the genius level."

The skiff veered wildly as Shearing dodged a whizzing chunk of rock the size of a skyscraper.

"That's one reason," he said, "why we wanted to get you before Bellaver did. The number of technicians undergoing the Humane Penalty is quite small. We—the brotherhood—need all of them we can get."

"But that wasn't the main reason you wanted me?" pressed Hyrst.

Shearing looked at him. "No. We wanted you mainly because you were present when MacDonald died. Handled right—"

He paused. The asteroid was rushing at them, and Bellaver's ships were close behind. Hyrst was already in a vac-suit, all but the helmet.

"Take the controls," said Shearing. "As she goes. Don't worry, I'll make the landing." He pulled the vac-suit on. "Handled right," he said, "you might be the key to that murder, and to the mystery behind it that the brotherhood *must* solve."

He took the controls again. They helped each other on with their helmets. The asteroid filled the port, a wild, weird jumble of vari-colored rock.

"I don't see how," said Hyrst, into his helmet mike.

"Latent impressions," answered Shearing briefly, and sent the skiff skittering in between two great black monoliths, to settle with a jar on a pan of rock as smooth and naked as a ballroom floor.

"Make it fast," said Shearing. "They're right on top of us."

THE SKIFF, designed as Sheering had said for short hops, could not accommodate the extra weight and bulk of an airlock. You were supposed to land in atmosphere. If you didn't, you just pushed a release-button and hung on. The air was exhausted in one whistling swoosh that took with it everything loose. The moisture in it crystallized instantly, and before this frozen drift had even begun to settle, Hyrst and Shearing were on their way.

They crossed the rock pan in great swaggering bounds. The gravity was light, the horizon only twenty or so miles away. Literally in his mind's eye Hyrst could see the three ships arrowing at them. He opened contact with Vernon, knowing Shearing had done so too. Vernon had been looking for them.

"Mr. Bellaver still prefers to have you alive," he said. "If you'll wait quietly beside the skiff, we'll take you aboard."

Shearing gave him a hard answer.

"Very well," said Vernon. "Mr. Bellaver wants me to make it clear to you that he doesn't intend for you to get away. So you can interpret that as you please. Be seeing you."

He broke contact, knowing that Hyrst and Shearing would close him out. From now on, Hyrst realized, he would keep track of them the way he and Shearing had kept track of obstructions in the path of flight, by mental "sight". The yacht was extremely close. Suddenly Hyrst had a confused glimpse of a hand on a control-lever over-lapped by a view of the black-mouthed tubes of the yacht's belly-jets. He dived, literally, into a crack between one of the monoliths and a slab that leaned against its base, dragging Shearing with him.

The yacht swept over. Nothing happened. It dropped out of sight, braking for a landing.

"Imagination," said Shearing. "You realize a possibility, and you think it's so. Tricky. But I don't blame you. The safe side is the best one."

Hyrst looked out the crack. One of the tugs was coming in to land beside the skiff, while the other one circled.

"Now what?" he said. "I suppose we can dodge them for a while, but we can't hide from Vernon."

Shearing chuckled. He had got his look of tough competence back. He seemed almost to be enjoying himself. "I told you, you were only a cub. How do you suppose we've kept the starship hidden all these years? Watch."

In the flick of a second Hyrst went blind and deaf. Then he realized that it was only his mental eyes and ears that were blanked out as though a curtain had been drawn across them. His physical eyes were still clear and sharp, and when Shearing's voice came over the helmet audio he heard it without trouble.

"This is called the cloak. I suppose you could call it an extension of the shield, though it's more like a force field. It's no bar to physical vision, and it has the one great disadvantage of being opaque both ways to mental energy. But it does act as a deflector. If Vernon follows us now, he'll have to do it the hard way. Stick close by me, so I don't have too wide a spread. And it'll be up to you to lead. I can't do both. Let's go."

Hyrst had, unconsciously, become so used to his new perceptions that it made him feel dull and helpless to be without them. He led off down one of the smooth rock avenues, going away from the skiff and the tug which had just landed.

On either side of the avenue were monoliths, irregularly spaced and of different sizes and heights but following an apparently orderly plan. The light of the distant sun lay raw and blinding on them, casting shadows as black and sharp-edged as though drawn upon the rock with india ink.

You could see faces in the monoliths. You could see mighty outlines, singly and in groups, of gods and beasts and men, in combat, in suppliance, in death and burial. That was why these asteroids were called Valhallas. Twenty-six of them had been found so far, and studied, and still no one could say certainly whether or not the hands of any living beings had fashioned them. They might be actual monuments, defaced by cosmic dust, by collision with the myriad fragments of the Belt, by time. They might be one of Nature's casual jokes, created by the same agencies. No actual tombs had been found, nor tools, nor definitely identifiable artifacts. But still the feeling persisted, in the airless silence of the avenues, that some passing race had paused and wrought for itself a memorial more enduring than its fame, and then gone on into the great galactic sea, never to return.

HYRST had never been on a Valhalla before. He understood why Shearing had not wanted to land and he wished now that they hadn't. There was something overwhelmingly sad and awesome about these leaning, towering figures of stone, moving forever in their lonely orbit, going nowhere, returning to nowhere.

Then he saw the second tug overhead. He forgot his daydreams. "They're going to act as a spotter," he said. Shearing grunted but did not speak. His whole mind was concentrated on maintaining the cloak. Hyrst stopped him still in the pitchy shadow under what might have been a kneeling woman sixty feet high. He watched the tug. It lazed away, circling slowly, and he did not think it had seen them. He could not any longer see the place where they had landed, but he assumed that by now the yacht had looped back and come in—if not there somewhere close by. They could figure on nine to eleven men hunting them, depending on whether they left the ships guarded or not. Either way, it was too many.

"Listen," he said aloud to Shearing. "Listen, I want to ask you. What you said about latent impressions—you think I might have seen and heard the killer even though I was unconscious?"

"Especially heard. Possible. With your increased power, and ours, impressions received through sense-channels but not recognized at the time or remembered later might be recovered." He shook his head. "Don't bother me."

"I just wanted to know," said Hyrst. He thought of his son, and the two daughters he hoped he would never see. He thought of Elena. It was too late to do anything for her, but the others were still living. So was he, and he intended to stay that way, at least until he had done what he set out to do.

"Old Bellaver was behind that killing, wasn't he? Old Quentin, this one's grandfather."

"Yes. Don't bother me."

"One thing more. Do we Lazarites live longer than men?"

Shearing gave him a curious, brief look. "Yes."

The tug was out of sight behind a massive rearing shape that seemed to clutch a broken ship between its paws. Symbolic, perhaps, of space? Who knew? Hyrst led Shearing in wild impala-like leaps across an open space, and into a narrow way that twisted, filled with darkness, among the bases of a group that resembled an outlandish procession following a king.

"How much longer?"

"Humane Penalty first came in a hundred and fourteen years ago, right? After Seitz' method was perfected for saving spacemen. I was one of the first they used it on."

"My God," said Hyrst. Yet, somehow, he was not as surprised as he might have been.

"I've aged," said Shearing apologetically. "I was only twenty-seven then."

They crouched, beside a humped shape like a gigantic lizard with a long tail. The tug swung overhead and slowly on.

Hyrst said, "Then it's possible the one who killed MacDonald is still alive?"

"Possible. Probable."

Hyrst bared his teeth, in what was not at all like a smile. "Good," he said. "That makes me happy."

They did not do any talking after that. They had had their helmet radios operating on practically no power at all, so that they couldn't be picked up outside a radius of a few yards, but even that might be too close, now that Bellaver's men had had time to get suited and fan out. They shut them off entirely, communicating by yanks and nudges.

FOR WHAT seemed to Hyrst like a very long time, but which was probably less than half an hour in measured minutes, they dodged from one patch of shadow to another, following an erratic course that Hyrst thought would lead them away from the ships. Once more the tug went over, slow, and then Hyrst didn't see it again. The idea that they might have given up occurred to him but he dismissed it as absurd. With the helmet mike shut off, the silence was beginning to get on his nerves. Once he looked up and saw a piece of cosmic debris smash into a monolith. Dust and splinters flew, and a great fragment broke off and fell slowly downward, bumping and rebounding, and all of it as soundless as a dream. You couldn't hear yourself walk, you couldn't hear anything but the roar of your own breathing and the pounding of your own blood. The grotesque rocky avenues could hide an army, stealthy, creeping—

There was a hill, or at least a higher eminence, crowned with what might have been the cyclopean image of a man stretched out on a noble catafalque, with hooded giants standing by in attitudes of mourning. It seemed like the best place to stop that Hyrst had seen, with plenty of cover and a view of the surrounding area. With luck, you might stay hidden there a long time. He jogged Shearing's elbow and pointed, and Shearing nodded. There was a wide, almost circular sweep of open rock around the base of the hill. Hyrst looked carefully for the tug. There was no sign of it. He tore out across the open, with Shearing at his heels.

The tug swooped over, going fast this time. It could not possibly have missed them. Shearing dropped the cloak with a grunt. "No use for that any more," he said. They bounded up the hillside and in among the mourning figures. The tug whipped around in a tight spiral and hung over the hill. Hyrst shook the sweat out of his eyes. His mind was clear again. The tug's skipper was babbling into his communicator, and in another place on the asteroid Hyrst could mentally see a thin skirmish line spread out, and in still another four men in a bunch. They all picked up and began to move, toward the hill.

Shearing said, nodding spaceward, "Our friends are on the way. If we can hold out—"

"Fat chance," said Hyrst. "They're armed, and all we've got is flare-pistols." But he looked around. His eyes detected nothing but rock, hard sunlight, and deep shadow, but his mind saw that one of the black blots at the base of the main block, the catafalque, was more than a shadow.

He slid into a crack that resembled a passage, being rounded rather than ragged. Shearing was right behind him. "I don't like this," he said, "but I suppose there's no help for it."

The crack led down into a cave, or chamber, too irregularly shaped to be artificial, too smoothly surfaced and floored to be natural. There was nothing in it but a block of stone, nine feet or so long and about four feet wide by five feet high. It seemed to be a natural part of the floor, but Hyrst avoided it. On the opposite, the sunward side, there was a small window-like aperture that admitted a ray of blinding radiance, sharply defined and doing nothing to illumine the dark on either side of it.

Vernon's thought came to them, hard, triumphant, peremptory. "Mr. Bellaver says you have ten minutes to come out. After that, no mercy."

CHAPTER FIVE

The minutes slid past, sections of eternity arbitrarily measured by the standards of another planet and having no relevance at all on this tiny whirling rock. The beam of light from the small aperture moved visibly across the opposite wall. Hyrst watched it, blinking. Outside, Bellaver's men were drawn up in a wide crescent across the hill in front of the catafalque. They waited.

"No mercy," said Hyrst softly. "No mercy, is it?" He bent over and began to loosen the clamps that held the lead weights to the soles of his boots.

"It isn't mercy we need," said Shearing. "It's time."

"How much?"

"Look for yourself."

Hyrst shifted his attention to space. There was a ship in it, heading toward the asteroid, and coming fast. Hyrst frowned, doing in his head without thinking about it a calculation that would have required a computer in his former life.

"Twenty-three minutes and seventeen seconds," he said, "inclusive of the four remaining."

He finished getting the weights off his boots. He handed one to Shearing. Then he half-climbed, half-floated up the wall and settled himself above the entrance, where there was a slight concavity in the rock to give him hold.

"Shearing," he said.

"What?" He was settling himself beside the mouth of the crack, where a man would have to come clear inside to get a shot at him.

"A starship implies the intention to go to the stars. Why haven't you?"

"For the simplest reason in the world," said Shearing bitterly. "The damn thing can't fly."

"But—" said Hyrst, in astonishment.

"It isn't finished. It's been building for over seventy years now, and a long and painful process that's been, too, Hyrst—doing it bit by bit in secret, and every bit having to be dreamed up out of whole cloth, and often discarded and dreamed up again, because the principle of a workable star-drive has never been formulated before. And it still isn't finished. It can't be finished, unless—"

He stopped, and both men turned their attention to the outside.

"Bellaver's looking at his chrono," said Hyrst. "Go ahead, we've got a minute."

Shearing continued, "unless we can get hold of enough Titanite to build the hyper-shift relays. Nothing else has a fast enough reaction time, and the necessary load-capacity. We must have burned out a thousand different test-boards, trying."

"Can't you buy it?" asked Hyrst. The question sounded reasonable, but he knew as he said it that it was a foolish one. "I mean, I know the stuff is scarcer than virtue and worth astronomical sums—that's what MacDonald was so happy about—but—"

"The Bellaver Corporation had a corner on the stuff before our ship was even thought of. That's what brought this whole damned mess about. Some of our people—not saying why they wanted it, of course—tried to buy some from Bellaver in the usual way, and one of them must have been incautious about his shield. Because a Lazarite working for Bellaver caught a mental hint of the starship, and the reason for the Titanite, and that was it. Three generations of Bellavers have been after us for the stardrive, and it's developed into a secret war as bitter as any ever fought on the battlefield. They hold all the Titanite, we hold the ship, and perhaps now you're beginning to see why MacDonald was killed, and why you're so important to both sides."

"Beginning to," said Hyrst. "But only beginning."

"MacDonald found a Titanite pocket. And as you know, a Titanite pocket isn't very big. One man can break the crude stuff, fill a sack with it, and tote it on his own back if he doesn't have a power-sled."

"MacDonald had a sled."

"And he used it. He cleaned out his pocket, afraid somebody else would track him to it, and he hid the wretched ore somewhere. Then he began to dicker. He approached the Bellaver Corporation, and we heard of it and approached *him*. He tried playing us off against Bellaver to boost the price, and suddenly he was dead and you were accused of his murder. We thought you really had done it, because no Titanite turned up, and we knew Bellaver hadn't gotten it from him. We'd watched too closely. It wasn't until some years later that one of our people learned that MacDonald had threatened a little too loudly to sell to us unless Bellaver practically tripled his offer—and of course Bellaver didn't dare do that. A price so much out of line even for Titanite would have stirred all the rival shipbuilders to unwelcome curiosity. So, we figured, Bellaver had had him killed."

"But what happened to the Titanite?"

"That," said Shearing, "is what nobody knows. Bellaver must have figured that if his tame Lazarites couldn't find where MacDonald had put it, we couldn't either. He was right. With all our combined mental probes and conventional detectors we haven't been able to track it down. And we haven't been able to find any more pockets, either. Bellaver Corporation got exclusive mineral rights to the whole damned moon. They even own the refinery now."

Hyrst shook his head. "Latent impressions or not, I don't see how I can help on that. If MacDonald had given the killer any clue—"

A BEAM of bright blue light no thicker than a pencil struck in through the mouth of the passage. It touched the side of the large stone block. The stone turned molten and ran, and then the beam flicked off, leaving a place that glowed briefly red. Shearing said, "I guess our ten minutes are up."

They were. For a second or two nothing more happened and then Hyrst saw something come sailing in through the crack. His mind told him what it was just barely in time to shut his eyes. There was a flash that dazzled him even through his closed lids, and the flash became a glare that did not lessen. Bellaver's men had tossed in a long-term flare, and almost at once someone followed it, in the hope of catching Hyrst and Shearing blinded and off guard. The eyes of Hyrst's mind, unaffected by light, clearly showed him the suited figure just below him, with its bubble helmet covered by a glare-shield. They directed him with perfect accuracy in the downward sweep of the lead weight he had taken from his boot, and which he still held in his hand. The bubble helmet was very strong, and the gravity very light, but the concussion was enough to drop the man unconscious. Just about thought Hyrst, what happened to me there in the hoist tower, when MacDonald died. Shearing, who had by now adjusted his own glare-shield stooped quickly and took the man's gun.

He said aloud, over the helmet communicator, "The next one that steps through here gets it. Do you hear that, Bellaver?"

Bellaver's voice answered. "Listen, Shearing, I was wrong. I admit it. Let's calm down and start over again. I——"

"Ten minutes ago it was no mercy."

"It's hard for me to behave reasonably about this business. You know what it means to me, what it meant to my father and *his* father. But I'm willing to do anything, Shearing, if you'll make a deal."

"I'll make a deal. Readily. Eagerly. Give back what your grandfather stole from us, and we'll call it square."

"Oh no we won't," said Hyrst grimly, breaking in. "Not until I find who killed MacDonald."

"All right," said Bellaver. "Wilson, break out the grenades."

The entire surface of Hyrst's body burst into a flaring sweat. For one panic-stricken second he wanted to rush out the crack pleading for mercy. Then he got his feet against the wall and pushed hard, and went plunging across the chamber in a sort of floating dive. Shearing got there at the same time and helped to pull him down. They huddled together on the floor, with the coffin-shaped block between them and the crack. Hyrst sent out a frantic mental call to hurry, directed at the spaceship of the brotherhood.

"They're all going to hurry," said Shearing. "Vernon has found the ship now. He's telling Bellaver. Here comes the grenade——"

Small round glittering thing of death, curving light and graceful through the airless gloom. It comes so slowly, and the flesh shrinks quivering upon itself until it is nothing more than a handful of simple fear. Outside the men are running away, and the one who has thrown the grenade from the cramped, constructing vantage of the crack is running after them, and Shearing is crying with his mind Will it to fall short, *will it to fall sh—*

There is a great brilliance, and the rock leaps, but there is not the slightest sound.

CHAPTER SIX

"The Ram, the Bull, the Heavenly Twins, And next the Crab the Lion Shine. The Virgin and the Scales—"

The old zodiacal rhyme was running through Hyrst's mind, and that was the only thing that was in his mind.

The Virgin and the Scales.

Yes. And she's very beautiful, too, thought Hyrst. But she shouldn't be *holding* the Scales. That's all wrong. The Scales come next, and then the Scorpion—Scorpio—and the Archer—Sagittarius—

And anyway they aren't scales, they're a pair of big golden stars, and she's putting them down, and they're melting together. There's only one of them, and it's not a star at all, really. It's a polished metal jug, reflecting the light, and—

The Virgin smiled. "The doctor said you were coming around. I brought you something to drink."

Reality returned to Hyrst with a rush. "You're Christina," he said, and tried to sit up. He was dizzy, and she helped him, and he said, "I guess it did fall short."

"What?"

"The grenade. The last thing I remember is Shearing— Wait. Where is Shearing?"

"Sitting up in the lounge, nursing his bruises. Yes, it fell short, but I don't think telekinetics had much to do with that. We've never been able to control matter convincingly. There. All right?"

"Fine. How did you get us out?"

"Of course the grenade had made the entrance impassable—we had to cut our way in through the outer wall. We had a clear field. Bellaver's men had all gone back to their ships. They thought you were dead, and to tell you the truth we thought you must be, too. But you didn't quite 'feel' dead, so we dug you out."

"Thanks," said Hyrst. "I suppose they know different now."

He was in a ship's sick-bay. From the erratic crash and shudder of the lateral jets, they were beating their way through the Belt, and at a high rate of speed. Hyrst sent a glance back into space. The tugs and Bellaver's yacht were following, but this time only the yacht had a chance. The tugs were dropping hopelessly behind.

"Yes, they soon found out once we got you out, but with any luck we'll lose them," said Christina. She sat down beside the bunk, where she could see his face. "Shearing told you about the ship."

"The starship. Yes." He looked at her. Suddenly he laughed. "You're not a goddess at all."

"Who said I was?"

"Shearing. Or anyway, his mind. Ten feet tall, and crowned with stars—I was afraid of you." He leaned closer. "Your eyes, though. They are angry."

"So will yours be," she said, "when you've fought the Bellavers as long as we have."

"There are still things I don't understand. Why you built the ship, why you've kept it secret from everyone, not just Bellaver, what you plan to do with it—how *you* came to be one of the Brotherhood."

She smiled. "The Seitz method was originated to save wreck-victims frozen in deep space. Remember? Quite a few of us never went through the door at all, innocent or guilty. But that makes no difference, once you've come back from out there." She put her hand on his. "You've learned fast, but you're only on the threshold. There's no need for words with us. Open your mind—"

HE DID so. At first it was no different from the contact he had had with Shearing's mind, or with Christina's before on the *Happy Dream*. Thoughts came to him clearly phrased—*You want to know why we built the ship, what we plan to do with it*—and it was only after some time that he realized the words had stopped and he was receiving Christina's emotions, her memories and opinions, her disappointments and her dreams, as simply and directly as though they were his own.

You haven't had time yet, they told him without words, to realize how alone you are. You haven't tried, as most of us do at first, to be human again, to fit yourself into life as though the gap of time was not there, as though nothing had changed. You haven't watched people getting old around you while you have hardly added a gray hair. You haven't had to move from one place to another, one job, one group of friends to another, because sooner or later they sense something wrong about you. You haven't had to hide your new powers as you would hide a disease because people would fear and hate you, perhaps even kill you, if they knew. That's why there is a brotherhood. And that's why we built the ship.

Symbol of flight. Symbol of freedom. A universe wide beyond imagining, thronging with many colored guns, with new worlds where men in a human society could build a society of their own. *No boundaries beyond which the mind cannot dare to go. All space, all time, all knowledge—free!*

Once more he saw those wide dark seas between the suns. His mind raced with hers through the cold-flaming nebulae, wheeled blinded and stunned past the hiving stars of Hercules, looked in eager fascination at the splendid spiral of Andromeda—no longer, perhaps, beyond reach, for what are time and space to the intangible forces of the mind?

Then that wild flight ceased, and instead there was a smaller vision, misty and only half realized, of houses and streets, a place where they could live and be what they were, openly and without fear.

Can you understand now, she asked him, *what they would think if they knew about the ship? Can you understand that they would be afraid to have us colonizing out there, afraid of what we might do?*

He understood. At the very least, if the truth were known, the Lazarites would never be free again. They would be taken and tested and examined and lectured about, legislated over, restricted, governed, and used. They might be fairly paid for their ship and whatever other advancements they might develop, but they would never be permitted to use them.

With sudden savage eagerness Hyrst said, "But first of all I must know who killed MacDonald. Shearing explained about the latent impressions. I'm ready."

She stood up, regarding him with grave eyes. "There's no guarantee it will work. Sometimes it does. Sometimes not."

Hyrst thought about the tired, gray-haired man who had stood at the foot of his bed. "It'll work. It's got to."

He added, "If it doesn't, I'll tear the truth out of Bellaver with my hands."

"It may come to that," she said grimly. "But we'll hope. Lie quiet. I'll make the arrangements."

An hour later Hyrst lay on the padded table in the middle of the sick-bay. The ship spun and whirled and leaped in a sort of insane dance, and Hyrst was strapped to the table to prevent his being thrown off. He had known that the ship was maneuvering in the thickest swarm area of the Belt with four pilots mind-linked and flying esper, trying to out-dare Bellaver. Two others were keeping Vernon blanked, and they hoped that either Bellaver himself or his radar-deflector system would give up. Hyrst had known this, but now he was no longer interested. He was barely conscious of the lurching of the ship. They had given him some sort of a drug, and he lay relaxed and pliant in a pleasant suspension of all worries, looking vaguely up at the faces that were bent over him. Finally he closed his eyes, and even they were gone.

HE WAS crossing the plain of methane snow with MacDonald, under the glowing Rings. At first it was all a little blurred, but gradually the memory cleared until he was aware of each tiny detail far more clearly than he had been at the time—the texture of the material from which MacDonald's suit was made, the infinitesimal shadow underscoring every roughness of the snow, the exact sensation of walking in his leaded boots, the whisper and whistle of his oxygen system. He quarreled again with MacDonald, not missing a word. He climbed with him into the tower of Number Three hoist and examined the signal lights, and sat down on the bench, smiling, to wait.

He sweated inside his suit. He would take a shower when he got back to quarters. He wished for a smoke. MacDonald's steady grumbling and cursing filled his helmet. He listened, enjoying it. Hope you bang yourself with your own clumsy hammer. And I wish you joy of your fortune. If you have as many friends rich as you had poor you won't have any. There was an itch under his left arm. He pressed the suit in with his right and wriggled his body against it. It didn't do any good. Damn suits. Damn Titan. Lucky Elena, back on Earth with the kids. Making good money, though. Won't be long before I can go back and live like a human being. Now his nose itched, and MacDonald was still grumbling. There was the faintest ghost of a sound and then *crack*, then nothing, dark, cold, sinking, very weak, gone. Nothing, nothing. I come to in the cold silence and look down the shaft at MacDonald and he is dead.

Go back a bit. Slow. That's right. Easy. Back to Elena and the kids.

Lucky Elena, in the sun and the warm sweet air. Lucky kids. But I'm lucky too. I can go back to them soon. My nose itches. Why does your nose always itch when you've got a helmet on, or your hands all over grease? Listen to MacDonald, damning the belt, damning the tools, damning everything in sight. Is that a footstep? The air is thin and poisonous, but it carries sound. Somebody coming behind me? Split second, no time to look or think. *Crack.* Cold. Dark. Nothing.

Let's go back again. Don't hurry. We've all the time in the world. Go back to the footsteps you heard behind you.

Almost heard. And then I black and cold. Heavy. Flat. Face heavy against helmet, cold. Lying down. Must get up, must get up, danger. Far away. Can't. MacDonald is screaming. Let the lift alone, what are you doing, Hyrst? Hyrst! Shut up, you greedy little man, and listen. You're not Hyrst—who are you? That doesn't matter. I know, you're from Bellaver. Bellaver sent you to steal the Titanite. Well, you won't get it. It's where nobody will ever get it unless I show them how. Good. That's good, MacDonald. That's what I wanted to know. You see, *we* don't need the Titanite.

MacDonald screams again and the lift goes down with a roar and a rattle of severed chain.

Heavy footsteps, shaking the floor by my head. Someone turns me over, speaks to me, bending close. Light is gray and strange. I try to rouse. I can't. The man is satisfied. He drops me and goes away, but I have seen his face inside his helmet. I hear him working on some metal thing with a tool. He is whistling a little under his breath. MacDonald is not screaming now. From time to time he whimpers. But I have seen the killer's face.

I have seen his face.

I have seen—

Take it easy, Hyrst. Take your time.

Elena is dead, and this is Christina bending over me.

I have seen the killer's face.

It is the face of Vernon.

CHAPTER SEVEN

There was Christina, and there was Shearing, and there were two more he did not know, leaning over him. The drug was wearing off a little, and Hyrst could see them more clearly, see the bitter disappointment in their eyes.

"Is that all?" Christina said. "Are you sure? Go back again—"

They took him back again, and it was the same.

"That's all MacDonald said? Then we're no closer to the Titanite than we were before."

Hyrst was not interested in the Titanite. "Vernon," he said. Something red and wild rose up in him, and he tried to tear away the straps that held him. "Vernon. I'll get him—"

"Later, Hyrst," said Shearing, and sighed. "Lie still a bit. He's on Bellaver's yacht, remember? Quite out of reach. Now think. MacDonald said, You won't get it, it's where nobody will ever get it—"

"What's the use?" said Christina, turning away. "It was a faint hope anyway. Dying men don't draw obliging maps for you." She sat down on the edge of a bunk and put her head in her hands. "We might as well give up. You know that."

One of the two Lazarites who had done the latent probe on Hyrst said with hollow hopefulness, "Perhaps if we let him rest a while and then go over it again—"

"Let me up out of here," said Hyrst, still groggy with the drug. "I want Vernon."

"I'll help you get him," said Shearing, "if you'll tell me what MacDonald meant when he said *nobody will ever get it unless I show them how.*"

"How the devil do I know?" Hyrst tugged at the straps, raging. "Let me up."

"But you knew MacDonald well. You worked with him and beside him for years."

"Does that tell me where he hid the Titanite? Don't be an ass, Shearing. Let me up."

"But," said Shearing equably, "he didn't say *where.* He said *how.*"

"Isn't that the same thing?"

"Is it? Listen. Nobody will ever get it unless I show them where. Nobody will ever get it unless I show them how."

Hyrst stopped fighting the straps. He began to frown. Christina lifted her head again. She did not say anything. The two Lazarites who had done the probe stood still and held their breath.

Shearing's mind touched Hyrst's stroking it as with soothing fingers. "Let's think about that for a minute. Let your thoughts move freely. MacDonald was an engineer. The engineer. Of the four, he alone knew every inch of the physical set-up of the refinery. So?"

"Yes. That's right. But that doesn't say where—Wait a minute, though. If he'd just shoved it in a crack somewhere in the mountains, he'd know a detector might find it, more easily than before it was dug. He'd have put it some where deep, deeper than he could possibly dig. Maybe in an abandoned mine?"

"No place," said Shearing, "is too deep for us to probe. We've examined every abandoned mine on that side of Titan. And it doesn't fit, anyway. No. Try again."

"He wouldn't have brought it back to the refinery. One of us would be sure to find it. Unless, of course—"

Hyrst stopped, and the tension in the sick-bay tightened another notch. The ship lurched sharply, swerved, and shot upward with a deafening thunder of rocket-blasts. Hyrst shut his eyes, thinking hard.

"Unless he put it in some place so dangerous that nobody ever went there. A place where even he didn't go, but which he would know about being the engineer."

"Can you think of any place that would answer that description?"

"Yes," said Hyrst slowly. "The underground storage bins. They're always hot, even when they're empty. Anything hidden near them would be blanketed by radiation. No detector would see anything but uranium. Probably even you wouldn't."

"No," said Shearing, looking amazed. "Probably we wouldn't. The radioactive disturbance would be too strong to get through, even if we were looking for something beyond it, which we weren't."

CHRISTINA had sprung up. Now she bent over Hyrst and said, "But is there a way it could have been done? Obviously, the Titanite couldn't have been put directly into the bin with the uranium—if nothing else, it would have been shipped out in the next tanker."

"Oh, yes," said Hyrst. "There would be several ways. I can think of a couple myself, and I've never even see the layout. The repair-lift shaft, I know, goes clear down to the feeder mechanism, and there's some kind of a system of dispersal tunnels and an emergency gadget that trips automatically to release a liquid-graphite damping material into them in case the radiation level gets too high. I don't remember that it ever did, but it's a safeguard. There'd be plenty of places to hide a lead box full of Titanite."

"*Unless I show them how*," repeated Shearing slowly, and began to undo the straps that held Hyrst to the table. "It has an ominous sound. I'll bet you that locating the Titanite will be child's play compared to getting it out. Well, we'll do what we can."

"The first thing," said Christina grimly, "is to get rid of Bellaver. If he has the slightest suspicion where we're headed he'll radio ahead and have all Titan alerted."

Hyrst, sitting up now on the edge of the table, hanging on against the lurching of the ship, said, "That's right—he owns the refinery now, doesn't he? Is it still working?"

"No. The mines around there played out, oh, ten, fifteen years ago. The activity's shifted to the north and east on the other side of the range. That is what may possibly give us a chance." Shearing staggered with Hyrst across the bucking deck and sat tailor-fashion in the bunk, his eyes intent. "Hyrst, I want you to remember everything you can about the refinery. The ground plan, exactly where the buildings are, the hoists, the landing field. Everything."

Hyrst said, showing the edges of his teeth, "When do I get Vernon?"

"You'll get him. I promise you."

"What about Bellaver? He's still behind us."

Shearing smiled. "That's Christina's job! Let her worry."

Hyrst nodded. He began to remember the refinery. Christina and the other two went out.

A short while later a number of things happened, violently, and in quick succession. The ship of the Lazarites, pursuing its wild and headlong course through the swarming debris of the Belt, was far ahead of Bellaver's yacht but still within instrument range. Apparently in desperation it plunged suddenly on a tangential course into a cluster of great jagged rocks all travelling together at a furious rate of speed. The cluster was perhaps two hundred miles across. The Lazarite ship twisted and turned, and then there was a swift bright flowering of flame, and then nothing.

"She's blown her tubes," said Bellaver exultantly, on the bridge of his yacht. The instruments had lost contact, chiefly because the cluster was so thick that it was impossible to separate one body from another.

Vernon said, "They're not blanking my mind any more. It stopped, like that."

But he was still doubtful.

"Can you locate the ship?" asked Bellaver.

"I'm trying."

Bellaver caught his arm. "Look there!"

There was a second, larger and more brilliant, flash of flame.

"They've hit an asteroid," he said. "They're done for."

"I can't locate them," Vernon said. "No ship, no wreckage. It could be a trick. They could be holding a cloak."

"A trick?" said Bellaver. "I doubt it. Anyway, we're running low on fuel, and I'm not going to go into that cluster and risk my own neck to find out. If by any chance they do come out again later on, we'll deal with them."

But they both watched the cluster until it had whirled on out of sight. And neither eye nor instrument nor Vernon's probing mind could distinguish any sign of life.

CHAPTER EIGHT

Titan lay below them in the Saturn-glow, under the fantastic glory of the Rings. A bitter, repellent world of jagged peaks and glimmering plains of poison snow. The tiny life-raft dropped toward it, skittering nervously as it hit the thin atmosphere. Hyrst clung hard to the handholds, trying not to retch. He was not habituated to space anyway, and the skiff had been bad enough. Now, without any hull around him and nothing but a curved shield in front of him, he felt like an ant on a flying leaf.

"I don't like it either." Shearing said. "But it gives us a fifty-fifty chance of getting through unnoticed. Radar usually isn't looking for anything so small."

"*I* understand all the reasons," Hyrst said. "It's my stomach that's obtuse."

He could make out the pattern of the refinery now, a million miles of vertigo below him. The Lazarite ship was somewhere up and out behind them, hiding in the Rings. The trick had worked with Bellaver out there in the Belt, and they hoped now that it would work with Bellaver's observers on Titan. There was no need for any fake explosions this time, to give the impression of destruction. Secrecy was the watch-word, all lights out and jet-blasts muffled to a spark. Later, when Hyrst and Shearing had accomplished their mission, the ship would drop down fast and take them off, with the Titanite, before any patrol craft would have time to arrive.

They hoped.

The buildings of the refinery were dark and cold, drifted out of shape by an accumulation of the thin, evil snow. The spider web of roads had faded from the plain, and the landing field was smooth and unmarked. Around its perimeter the six stiff towers of the hoists stood up like lonely sentinels, hooded and cloaked.

Hyrst felt a sudden tightening of his throat, and this was a thing he had not expected. A refinery on Titan was hardly a thing to be sentimental about. But it was bound up so intimately with other things, with hopes for a future that was now far behind him, with plans for Elena and the kids that were now a cruel mockery, with friendly memories of Saul and Landers, now long dead, that he could not look at it unmoved.

"Let's try again," said Shearing quietly. "If we could locate the Titanite definitely it might make all the difference. We'll hardly have time to search all six of the bins."

Glad of the distraction, Hyrst tried. He linked his mind to Shearing's and they probed with this double probe, one after the other, the six hoists and the bins beneath them, while the raft fell whistling down the air.

It was the same as all the tries before. The bins had been empty for more than a decade, but the residual radiation was still hot enough to present a luminous haze to the eyes of the mind, fogging everything around it.

"Wait a minute," Hyrst said. "Let's use our wits. Look at the way those hoists are placed, in a wide crescent. Now if I was MacDonald, coming in from the mountains with a load of Titanite, and I wanted not to be seen, which one would I pick?"

"Either One or Six," said Shearing, without hesitation. "They're the farthest away from the buildings."

"But Number Six is at the west end of the crescent, and to reach it you would have to go clear across the landing field." He pointed mentally to Number One. "I'll bet on that one. Shall we give it another try?"

They did. This time, for a fleeting second, Hyrst thought he had something.

"So did I," said Shearing. "Sort of down under and *behind*."

"Yes," said Hyrst. "*Look* out!" His involuntary cry was caused by the sudden collision of the life-raft with a cloud. The vapor was very thick, and after the cruel clarity of space it made Hyrst feel that he was smothering. Shearing jockeyed the raft's meager controls, and in a minute or two they were below the cloud and spiraling down toward the landing field. It was snowing.

"Good," said Shearing. "We'll hope it keeps up."

THEY LANDED close to Number One Hoist and floundered rapidly through the shallow drifts, carrying some things. The hatch had been sealed with a plastic spray to prevent corrosion, and it took them several minutes to get it open. Inside the tower it was pitch black, but they did not need lights. Their other senses showed them the worn metal treads of the steps quite clearly. In the upper chamber the indicator panels were dark and dead. Hyrst shivered inside his suit. He had been here so many times before, so long ago.

"Let's get busy," Shearing said.

They pulled on the rayproofs they had brought with them from the raft. Without power the lift was useless, but the skeleton cage, stripped of all its tools, was not too heavy for two strong men to swing clear of the shaft top. They made sure it would stay clear, and then sent down a light collapsible ladder. Hyrst slid down first into the smooth, round, totally unlighted hole, that had one segment of it open paralleling the machinery of the hoist.

"Take it carefully," Shearing said, and slid after him.

Clumsy in vac-suit and rayproof, Hyrst descended the ladder with agonizing slowness. Every impulse cried out for haste, but he knew if he hurried he would wind up at the bottom of the shaft as dead as MacDonald. The banging and knocking of their passage against the metal wall made a somber, hollow booming in that enclosed space, and it seemed to Hyrst that the silent belts and cables of the hoist hummed a little in sympathy. It was probably only the blood humming in his own ears.

"See anything yet?"

"No."

The vast strange glowing of the bin grew brighter as they approached it. The hoist was still "hot," and it glowed too, but nothing like the concentration in the bin.

"Even with rayproofs, we can't stay close to that too long."

"I don't think we'll have to. MacDonald was only human, and the bin was full then. He couldn't have stayed long either."

"See anything yet?"

"Nothing but fog. When you hit bottom, better use your light."

At long last Hyrst felt the bottom of the shaft under his boots. He stood aside from the ladder and switched on his belt lamp. In this case the physical eyes were better than the mental, being insensitive to radiation. Instantly the gears and cams of the feeder assembly sprang into sharp relief on the open side of the shaft. Shearing stumbled down off the ladder and switched on his own light.

"Where was it we thought we saw something?"

"Down under and behind." Hyrst turned slowly around, questing. The shaft was unbroken except by the repair opening. He climbed through it, with some difficulty, because nobody was supposed to climb through it and the machinery was placed for easy access with extension tools from the lift. The bin itself was now directly opposite them, a big hopper cut deep in the solid rock and serving the feeder by simple gravity. The feeder pretty well filled its own rocky chamber. A place might have been found beside it for something not too big, but the first man who came down on the lift would have seen it whether he was looking for it or not.

Shearing pointed. A dark opening pierced the rock at one side. Hyrst tried to see into it with his mental eyes, but the "fog" was so dense and bright—

He saw it, an unsubstantial ghostly shadow, but there. A square box some twenty feet down the tunnel.

Shearing drew a quick sharp breath "Let's go."

They went into the tunnel, crouching, scraping against the narrow sides.

"Look out for booby traps."

"I don't see any—yet."

The box sat in the middle of the tunnel. There was no way to get around it, no way to see over it without lying on its top and wriggling between it and the low roof. Hyrst and Shearing shut their eyes.

"I'm not sure, but I think I see a wire. Damn the fog. Can't tell where it goes—"

HYRST TOOK cutters from his belt and slithered cautiously over the box. His heart was hammering very hard and his hand shook so that he had great difficulty getting the cutters and the wire together. The wire was attached to the back of the box, very crudely and hastily attached with a blob of plastic solder. It was not until he had pinched the wire with the sharp metal cutter-teeth that he realized the plastic was non-metallic and the wire bare. And then, of course, it was too late.

There must have been a simple energizer somewhere up ahead, still charging itself from the ample radiation source. The cutters flew out of Hyrst's hand in a shower of sparks, and in the darkness of the tunnel ahead there was a sudden wild flare of light, and an explosion of dust. A shock wave, not too great, hammered past Hyrst's helmet. Shearing yelled once, a protest broken short in mid-cry. Then they waited.

The dust settled. The brief tremor of the rock was stilled.

In the roof of the tunnel, where the blast had been, a broken dump-trap hung open, but nothing poured out of it but a handful of black dust.

Hyrst began to laugh. He lay on his belly on top of the box of Titanite and laughed. The tears ran out of his eyes and down his nose and dropped onto the inside of his helmet. Shearing hit him from behind. He hit him until he stopped laughing, and then Hyrst shook his head and said.

"Poor MacDonald."

"Yeah. Go ahead, you can cut the wire now."

"Such a lovely booby trap. But he wasn't figuring on time. They went away from here, Shearing, you see? And when they went they drained off the liquid graphite and took it with them. So there isn't anything left to flood the tunnel. Pathetic, isn't it?"

Shearing hit him again. "Cut the wire."

He cut it. They scuffled backward down the tunnel, dragging the box. When they got back into the shaft where there was room to do it they opened up the box.

"Doesn't look like much, does it, for all the trouble it's made?"

"No, it doesn't. But then gold doesn't look like much, or uranium, or a handful of little dry seeds." Shearing picked up a chunk of the rough, grayish ore. "You know what that is, Hyrst? That's the stars."

It was Hyrst's turn to prod Shearing into quiet. The starship and the dream that went with it were still only an intellectual interest to him. They shared out the Titanite into two webbing sacks. It made a light load for each, hardly noticeable when clipped to a belt-ring at the back.

Hyrst felt suddenly very nervous. Perhaps it was reaction, perhaps it was the memory of having been trapped in a similar hole on the Valhalla asteroid. Perhaps it was a mental premonition, obscured by the radioactive "fog". At any rate, he started to climb the ladder with almost suicidal haste, urging Shearing on after him. The shaft seemed to be a mile high. It seemed to lengthen ahead of him as he climbed, so that he was never any nearer the top. He knew it was only imagination, because he passed the level markers, but it was the closest thing to a nightmare he had ever experienced when he was broad awake. Just after they had passed the E Level mark, Shearing spoke.

"A ship has landed."

Hyrst looked mentally. The fog-effect was not so great now, and he could see quite clearly. It was a small ship, and two men were getting out of it. It had stopped snowing.

"Radar must have picked up the raft after all," said Shearing. "Or else somebody spotted the jet-flares." He began to climb faster. "We better get out of this before they come in."

D Level. Hyrst's hands were cold and stiff inside his gauntlets, clumsy hooks to catch the slender rungs. The two men were standing outside in the snow, peering around.

C Level. One of the two men saw the raft parked by the hoist tower. He pointed, and they moved toward it.

B Level. Hyrst's boots slipped and scrambled, banging the shaft wall. "Christ," said Shearing. "You sound like a temple gong. What are you trying to do, alarm the whole moon?"

THE MEN outside bent over the raft. They looked at it. Then they looked at the hoist tower. They left the raft and began to run, pulling guns out of their belts.

A Level. Hyrst's breath roared in his helmet like a great wind. He thought of the long dark way down that was below them, and how MacDonald had looked at the bottom of the shaft, and how he would take Shearing with him if he fell, and nobody would get to the stars, and Vernon would go free. He set his teeth, and sobbed, and climbed. Outside, the two men cautiously removed the hatch and stepped into the tower.

End of the ladder. A level floor to sprawl on. Hyrst squirmed away from the shaft. He thought for a minute he was going to pass out, and he fumbled with the oxygen valve, making the mixture richer. His head began to clear. Shearing was now beside him. This time they had guns, too. Shearing gave him a quick mental caution, *Not unless you have to*. One of the two men was placing a tentative foot on the stair that led up to where they were. The other man was close behind him. Shearing took careful aim and fired, at half power.

The harsh blue bolt did not strike either man. But they went reeling back in a cloud of burning flakes, and when Shearing shouted to them to drop their weapons and get out they did so, half stunned from the shock. Hyrst and Shearing leaped down the stairs, stopping only long enough to pick up the guns. Then they scrambled outside. The two men were running as hard as they could for their ship, but they had not gone far and Shearing stopped them with another shot that sent a geyser of methane steam puffing up practically under their feet.

"Not yet," he said. "Later."

The two men stood, sullenly obedient. They were both young, and not bad looking. Just doing a job, Hyrst thought. No real harm in them, just doing a job, like so many people who never stop to worry about what the job means. They both wore Bellaver's insigne on their vac-suits.

One of them said, as though he were reciting a lesson in which he had no real personal interest, "You're trespassing on private property. You'll be prosecuted to the fullest extent of the law."

"Sure," said Shearing. He motioned to the hoist tower. "Back inside."

The young men hesitated. "What you going to do?"

"Nothing fatal. It shouldn't take you more than half an hour to break out again."

He marched them to the hatch and saw them inside it. Hyrst was watching the sky, the black star-glittering sky with the glorious arch of the Rings across it and one milky-bright curve of Saturn visible and growing above the eastern horizon.

"They're coming," he said mentally to Shearing.

"Good." He started to close the hatch, and one of the young men pointed suddenly to the sack clipped to Shearing's belt.

"You've been stealing something."

"Tell that to Bellaver."

"You bet I will. The fullest extent of the law, mister! The fullest extent—"

The hatch closed. Shearing jammed the fastening mechanism so it could not be turned from the inside. Then he went and stood beside Hyrst in the glimmering plain, watching the ship drop down out of the Rings.

Hyrst said, "They'll tell Bellaver."

"Naturally."

"What will Bellaver do?"

"I'm not sure. Something drastic. He wants our starship so hard he'd murder his own children to get it. You can see why. In itself it's priceless, a hundred years ahead of its time, but that's not all. It's what it stands for. To us it means freedom and safety. To Bellaver it means—"

He gestured toward the sky, and Hyrst nodded, seeing in Shearing's mind the image of a gigantic Bellaver, ten times bigger than God, gathering the whole galaxy into his arms.

"I wish you luck," said Hyrst. He unhooked the sack of Titanite from his belt and gave it to Shearing. "It'll take a little while to refine the stuff and build the relays, even so. That may be time enough. Come back for me if you can."

"Vernon?"

"Yes."

Shearing nodded. "I said I'd help you get him. I will."

"No. This is my job. I'll do it alone. You belong there, with them. With Christina."

"Hyrst. Listen—"

"Don't tell me where the starship is. I might not hold out as well as you."

"All right, but Hyrst—in case we can't get back—look for us away from the Sun. Not toward it."

"I'll remember."

The ship landed. Shearing entered it, carrying the Titanite. And Hyrst walked away, toward the closed and buried buildings of the refinery.

It had begun to snow again.

CHAPTER NINE

It was cold and dark and infinitely sad. Hyrst wandered through the rooms, feeling like a ghost, thinking like one. Everything had been removed from the buildings. The living quarters were now mere cubicular tombs for a lot of memories, absolutely bare of any human or familiar touch. It felt very strange to Hyrst. He kept telling himself that fifty years had passed, but he could not believe it. It seemed only a few months since MacDonald's death, months occupied by investigation and trial and the raging, futile anguish of the unjustly accused. The long interval of the pseudo-death was no more than a night's sleep, to a mind unconscious of passing time. Now it seemed that Saul and Landers should still be here, and there should be lights and warmth and movement.

There was nothing. He could not bring himself to stay in the living quarters. He went into one of the storerooms and sat on a concrete buttress and waited. It was a long and dreadful wait. During it all the emotional storms occasioned by the murder and its aftermath passed through his mind. Scenes with Saul and Landers. Scenes with the investigators, with MacDonald's family, with lawyers and reporters. Scenes with Elena. The whole terrible nightmare, leading inevitably to that culminating moment when the door of the airlock opened and he joined the sleepers on the plain. When it was all over Hyrst felt shaken and exhausted, but calm. The face of Vernon burned brightly in his mind's eye.

Without bothering to open the steel-shuttered windows, he watched the two young men force their way out of the hoist tower. He watched them run to their ship and chatter excitedly over their radio. By the time, much later, that Bellaver's yacht came screaming down to the landing field on a flaming burst of jets, he could watch it with almost the cool detachment of a spectator. He was careful to keep his shields up tight against Vernon, and he did not think the other Lazarite would be likely to look for him. Vernon seemed to be fully occupied with Bellaver.

"What else would they be stealing, you fool? You should have, killed Hyrst before, when you had the chance."

"Somebody had to take the blame for MacDonald. Anyway, you had him aboard the Happy Dream. *Why didn't you hang onto him?"*

"Don't get insolent with me, Vernon. I can turn you over to the police anytime, for any one of a hundred things."

"Not without tipping your hand, Bellaver."

"It would be worth it." A string of foul names, delivered in a furious scream. *"You couldn't locate the Titanite, but they did, just as soon as they got hold of Hyrst."*

"All right, Mr. God Almighty Bellaver, turn me in. But if it was the Titanite they took, you haven't a chance of finding that starship without me."

"You haven't done very well at it so far."

"In the excitement, they may get careless. But it's up to you."

More foul language, but Bellaver did not repeat his threat. He and Vernon, with a couple of other men, got into vac-suits and lumbered across the snow to the hoist tower. From inside the cold dark buried building, Hyrst watched them, and thought hard and fast, and smiled. Presently he left the building and circled cautiously through the snowy gloom until he was in range of their helmet-communicators. He could hear them aurally now, but he kept watching them, esper-fashion.

THEY inspected the empty lead box, and the young men told what had happened, and Bellaver turned his raging fury against them. There was no longer any doubt that the Titanite had been found and taken away, and Bellaver saw the stars and worlds and moons, the bright glowing plunder of a galaxy, slipping away from him. He threatened the two young men with every punishment he could think of for not having stopped the thieves, and one of the young men turned white and anxious, and the other one flushed brick red and shook his fist close to Bellaver's helmet.

"You go to hell," he said. "I don't care who you are. You go to hell."

He walked out of the hoist tower, with his companion stumbling at his heels, and Bellaver screamed after them, and behind him the crewmen looked shocked and contemptuous, and Vernon laughed openly, showing the edges of his teeth.

The two young men got into their ship and went away. Bellaver turned and stood looking at the empty box. He seemed exhausted now, hopeless, like a child about to break down and cry. Vernon went over and kicked the box.

"Hyrst had the advantage," he said. "He knew MacDonald and he knew the refinery. Even so, it must have been pure guesswork. Nobody could probe through that fog."

"What are we going to do?" asked Bellaver. "Vernon, what are we going to do?"

Hyrst spoke for the first time, his voice ringing loud and startling in their ears.

"Don't ask Vernon," he said. "Ask me."

There was a moment of complete silence. Hyrst felt Vernon's mind brush his, and he permitted himself one cruel flash of triumph. Then everybody spoke at once, Vernon explaining why he hadn't spotted Hyrst—who could have figured he'd stay behind at a time like this?— the crew-members nervously fingering their guns, and Bellaver crying,

"Hyrst! Is that you, Hyrst? Where are you?"

"Where I can get the first shot at anybody coming out of the tower, and where nobody from the yacht will ever reach me. Tell them all to stay put. Go ahead, Bellaver, you want to hear me out, don't you?"

"What do you want to say?"

"I can find you that starship. Tell them, Bellaver."

He told them. And Vernon said to Bellaver, "If he's willing to betray his friends, why would he get them the Titanite?" He laughed. "It isn't even a good trick."

"Oh, yes, it is," said Hyrst softly. "It's a very good one. The best. You see, I don't care about the starship or the Titanite. All I care about is the man who killed MacDonald. They were sort of bound up together. Ever hear of latent impressions, Vernon? I was unconscious, but my ears heard and my eyes saw, and my brain remembered, when it was shown how."

"That was fifty years ago," said Vernon. "People don't understand about us. Nobody would believe you if you told them."

"They would if Bellaver told them. They would if Bellaver explained out loud about the Lazarites, about what happens to men when they go through the door. They'd listen to him. And there must be others who know, or at least suspect." Hyrst paused, long enough to smile. "The beauty of that is, Bellaver, that you're in the clear. You're not responsible for a murder your grandfather had done. You could swear you didn't even know about it until now."

Vernon said to Bellaver, "If you do this to me, I'll blast you wide open."

"What can he do, Bellaver?" Hyrst shouted. "He can talk, but you have the money, the position, the legal powers. You can talk louder. And when they know the truth, will anybody take the word of a Lazarite against a human man?"

His voice rose higher and louder, drowning out Vernon's cry.

"Are you afraid of him, Bellaver? Are you so afraid of him you'll let the starship go?"

"Hold him." Bellaver said, and the crewmen held Vernon fast. "Wait a minute, Hyrst," he said. "What's your angle? Is it just revenge? Are you selling out your friends for something over and done half a century ago? I don't believe it, Hyrst."

Hyrst said slowly, "I can answer that, so even you will understand. I have children. They're getting old now. They've lived all their lives thinking their father killed a man, not for love or for justice or in self-defense, but for sheer cold-blooded greed. I want them to know it wasn't so."

"Hold him!" Bellaver said. The crewmen struggled with Vernon, and Vernon said viciously to Bellaver,

"He'll never lead you to the starship. I can read his mind. When you've turned me in and blackened your grandfather's name to clear him, he'll laugh in your face. What are you, Bellaver, a fool?"

"Am I, Hyrst?"

"That's for you to find out. I'm offering you the starship for Vernon, and that's fair enough, because I want him as bad as you want it. And I can tell you, Bellaver, if you decide to play it smart and call in your guards to hunt me down, it will do you no good. I won't be alive when they take me."

Silence. In his mind's eye Hyrst could see the beads of sweat running down Bellaver's face behind his helmet. He could see Vernon's face, too. It gave him pleasure.

"It should be an easy decision, Bellaver," he said. "After all, suppose I am lying. What have you got to lose but Vernon? And with his record, that isn't much."

"Hold him," said Bellaver. "All right, Hyrst. I'll do it. But I'll tell you now. If you lie to me, there won't be any re-awakening in another fifty years. This will be for good."

"Fair enough," said Hyrst. "I'm putting my gun away. I'm coming in."

He walked quickly through the snow toward the tower.

CHAPTER TEN

On the bridge of his yacht, Bellaver turned to Hyrst and said,

"I've done what you wanted. Now find me that starship."

Hyrst nodded. "Take off."

The rockets roared and thundered, and the swift yacht leaped quivering into the sky.

Hyrst sat quietly in his recoil chair. He felt a different man, changed entirely in the last few days. Much had happened in those days.

Bellaver had got busy on the radio even before his yacht left Titan, and the story of the Lazarites had burst like a nova upon the Solar System. Already there were instances of suspected Lazarites being mobbed by their neighbors, and Government was frantically concerning itself with all the new, far-reaching implications of the Humane Penalty.

Close on the heels of this bomb-shell had come Vernon's angry accusations against Bellaver, delivered as soon as he was given to the authorities on Mars. During the twenty Martian hours necessary for formal charge and the taking of depositions, and while Bellaver's yacht was being refueled, Vernon's story of the starship went out on all the interworld circuits. And it had been as Christina had said. The whole Solar System was frantic to have the Lazarites caught and stopped, and every man in space became a self-appointed searcher for the hidden starship. Bellaver, letting his lawyers worry about Vernon's accusations, had already laid formal claim to that ship, based on the value of the stolen Titanite.

"Where?" demanded Bellaver now, in a fury of impatience. "Where?"

"Wait," said Hyrst. "There are too many watching, ready to follow you. They know what you're after. Wait till we're clear of Mars."

He sat in his chair, looking into space. His drive was all gone, and the anger that had fed it. Somewhere his son and his two daughters were drawing their first free breaths relieved of a burden they should never have had to carry. They knew now that he was innocent, and they could think of him now without bitterness, speak his name without hate. He had done what he had set out to do, and he was finished. He knew what was ahead of him, but he was too tired to care.

The yacht went fast, away from the old red weary planet. Hyrst thought of Shearing and Christina and the others, laboring over their ship on the dark plain. He felt safe in doing this, because Vernon was gone and the gray evil man who had helped to torture Shearing aboard the *Happy Dream* was still in an Earth hospital recovering from the blow Hyrst had given him. They were out of reach, and Hyrst was the only Lazarite Bellaver had.

He did not try to get through to Shearing because he knew that was impossible, and there was no reason for it anyway. He let his mind stretch out and rove through the nighted spaces beyond Saturn, beyond Uranus and Neptune, beyond the black and frigid bulk of Pluto. He did not see the ship nor touch a Lazarite mind, and so he knew that they were still holding the cloak, still hiding from possible betrayal. He withdrew his mind, and wished them luck.

"We're clear of Mars," said Bellaver. "Which way?"

"That way," said Hyrst, and pointed. "Toward the Sun."

The yacht swerved and steadied on a new course, toward the distant glare of Sol. And Bellaver said,

"What's the exact location?"

"Can you trust every man in this crew?" asked Hyrst. "Can you be sure not one of them would give it away, when we stop to refuel? You're not the only one that knows about the starship now, remember."

"You could tell *me*."

"You're too impatient, Bellaver. You'd want to head straight there, and it won't be that easy. They have defenses. We have to be careful, or they'll destroy the ship before we reach it."

"Or finish their relays and go." Bellaver gave Hyrst a long look. "I'll trust you because I have to. But I wasn't making an empty threat. And I'll do it so there won't be any thought of murder. You'd better find me that ship, Hyrst."

From then on, Bellaver hardly slept. He paced the corridors and haunted the control room and watched Hyrst with a gnawing, agonizing doubt. Hyrst began to feel for him a distant sort of pity, as he might have felt for a man afflicted by some disease brought on by his own excesses.

THE YACHT passed the orbit of Earth, refueled at an obscure space station, and sped on. Hyrst continued to stall Bellaver, ordering a change of course from time to time to keep him happy. At intervals he let his mind rove through those dark spaces they were leaving farther behind with every passing second. Each time it was a greater effort, but still there was no sign of the starship or its base, and so he knew that the labor still went on.

By the time the yacht reached the orbit of Venus a fan-shaped cordon of other ships had collected around and behind her drawn by the word that Bellaver was on his way to find the starship. Government patrols were in constant touch.

"They can't interfere," said Bellaver. "I've got a lien on that ship, a formal claim."

"Sure," said Hyrst. "But you'd better be the first to find it. Possession, you know. Bear off a bit. Mislead them. They're sure now they know where you're going."

"Don't they?" said Bellaver, looking ahead at the glittering spark that was Mercury. "There isn't anyplace else to go."

"Isn't there?"

Bellaver stared at him, narrow-eyed. "The legend of the Vulcan was exploded by the first explorers. There is no intra-Mercurial world."

Hyrst shot a swift stabbing mental glance toward Pluto. Still nothing. He sighed and said easily,

"There wasn't then. There is now."

He brazened out the look of incredulity on Bellaver's face.

"These are Lazarites, remember, not men. They built a place for themselves where nobody would ever think to look. Not a planet, of course, just a floating workshop. A satellite. And now you know. So you can let them beat you to Mercury."

"All right," said Bellaver softly. "All right."

They passed Mercury, lost in the blaze of the Sun, and only a few ships followed them, far behind. The rest stopped to search the craggy valleys of the Twilight Belt, and the bleak ice fields of the Dark Side.

And now Hyrst had run his string out, and he knew it. When no intra-Mercurial satellite showed up, physically or on detector-screens, there was no further lie to tell. He drove his mind out and away, to the cold planets wheeling on the fringes of Sol's light, and he sweated, and prayed, and hoped that nothing had gone wrong. And suddenly the cloak was dropped, and he saw a lonesome chip of rock beyond Pluto, all hollowed out for shops and living quarters, and the great ship standing in the mile-long plain, with the stars all drifted overhead. And the ship lifted from the plain, circled upward, and suddenly was not.

Hyrst was bitterly sorry that he was not aboard. But he told Bellaver, "You can stop looking now. They've got away."

He watched Bellaver die, standing erect on his feet, still breathing, but dying inside with the last outgoing of hope.

"I thought you were lying," he said, "but it was the only chance I had." He nodded, looking toward the shuttered port with the insufferable blaze outside. He said, in a flat, dead voice, "If you were put out here, bound, in a lifeboat, headed toward the Sun—Yes. I could make up a story to fit that."

In the same toneless voice, he called his men. And suddenly the yacht lurched over shuddering in the backwash of some tremendous energy. Hyrst and the others were flung scattering against the bulk-heads, and the lights went out, and the instruments went dead.

Beyond the port, on the unshuttered side away from the Sun, a vast dark shape had materialized out of nothing, to hang close in space beside the yacht.

Hyrst heard in his mind, strong and clear, the voice of Shearing saying, "Didn't I tell you the brotherhood stands by its own? Besides, we couldn't make a liar out of you, now could we?"

Hyrst began to laugh, just a little bit hysterically. He told Bellaver, "There's your starship. And Shearing says if I'm not alive when he comes aboard to get me, that they won't be as careful about warping space when they go away as they were when they came."

Bellaver did not say anything. He sat on the deck where the shock had thrown him, not speaking. He was still sitting there when Hyrst passed through the airlock into the starship's boat, and he did not move even when the great ship vanished silently into whatever mysterious ultra-space the minds of the Lazarites had unlocked, outbound for the limitless freedom of the universe, where the wheeling galaxies thunder on forever across infinity and the stars burn bright, and there is nothing to stop the march of the Legion of Lazarus. And who knew, who could tell, where that march would end?

Aboard the starship, already a million miles away, Hyrst said to Christina. "When they brought me back from beyond the door, that was re-awakening. But this—this is being born again."

She did not answer that. But she took his hand and smiled.

THE END

If you've enjoyed this book, you will not want to miss these terrific titles...

ARMCHAIR SCI-FI & HORROR DOUBLE NOVELS, $12.95 each

D-21 **EMPIRE OF EVIL** by Robert Arnette
THE SIGN OF THE TIGER by Alan E. Nourse & J. A. Meyer

D-22 **OPERATION SQUARE PEG** by Frank Belknap Long
ENCHANTRESS OF VENUS by Leigh Brackett

D-23 **THE LIFE WATCH** by Lester del Rey
CREATURES OF THE ABYSS by Murray Leinster

D-24 **LEGION OF LAZARUS** by Edmond Hamilton
STAR HUNTER by Andre Norton

D-25 **EMPIRE OF WOMEN** by John Fletcher
ONE OF OUR CITIES IS MISSING by Irving Cox

D-26 **THE WRONG SIDE OF PARADISE** by Raymond F. Jones
THE INVOLUNTARY IMMORTALS by Rog Phillips

D-27 **EARTH QUARTER** by Damon Knight
ENVOY TO NEW WORLDS by Keith Laumer

D-28 **SLAVES TO THE METAL HORDE** by Milton Lesser
HUNTERS OUT OF TIME by Joseph E. Kelleam

D-29 **RX JUPITER SAVE US** by Ward Moore
BEWARE THE USURPERS by Geoff St. Reynard

D-30 **SECRET OF THE SERPENT** by Don Wilcox
CRUSADE ACROSS THE VOID by Dwight V. Swain

ARMCHAIR SCIENCE FICTION CLASSICS, $12.95 each

C-7 **THE SHAVER MYSTERY, Book One**
by Richard S. Shaver

C-8 **THE SHAVER MYSTERY, Book Two**
by Richard S. Shaver

C-9 **MURDER IN SPACE** by David V. Reed
by David V. Reed

ARMCHAIR MASTERS OF SCIENCE FICTION SERIES, $16.95 each

M-3 **MASTERS OF SCIENCE FICTION, Vol. Three**
Robert Sheckley, "The Perfect Woman" and other tales

M-4 **MASTERS OF SCIENCE FICTION, Vol. Four**
Mack Reynolds, "Stowaway" and other tales

TREASURE HUNT ON A PLANET OF ALIEN SURPRISES...

Ras Hume had set out with his civ clients on a big-game safari on Jumala. This was going to be a hunting party, but what they were really sent to find was known only to Hume. For somewhere in that other-world jungle, a man—reconditioned with another man's brain patterns—was planted. Whoever located this supposed lone survivor of a spaceship crash would receive an enormous reward. Unfortunately, planting Vye Lansor was a mistake. Something was wrong, because if their brainwashed quarry couldn't guess exactly what was going on, he knew that parts of his past were showing behind that conditioned barrier. But there was an even bigger mistake in Hume's schemes. And it would rapidly lead to the hunters becoming the hunted—with little chance of escape!

ABOUT ANDRE NORTON

Andre Norton...

...who sometimes wrote under the pseudonymn, Andrew North, attained a very favored status with science fiction readers from the 1950s right up until the time of her death in 2005. In a field that is still dominated primarily by men, Andre (Alice Mary) Norton stood out as one of the very best. Born in 1912, she was a native of Cleveland, Ohio and a life-long fan of science fiction and fantasy. Although most of her novels were first published in hardback editions, it is her paperback Ace Editions that seem to be best remembered. Some of her finest novels—all of which are considered classics—are *Witch World, The Last Planet, The Time Traders, Daybreak: 2250 A.D., The Stars are Ours, Star Gate, The Crossroads of Time, Mirror of Destiny, Judgment on Janus,* and many, many others. She was twice nominated for Hugo Awards and received the World Fantasy Award for lifetime achievement in 1998.

STAR HUNTER

By
ANDRE NORTON

ARMCHAIR FICTION
PO Box 4369, Medford, Oregon 97501-0168

*For more information about Armchair Books and products, visit our
website at…*

www.armchairfiction.com

Or email us at…

armchairfiction@yahoo.com

CHAPTER ONE

Nahuatl's larger moon pursued the smaller, greenish globe of its companion across a cloudless sky in which the stars made a speckled pattern like the scales of a huge serpent coiled around a black bowl. Ras Hume paused at the border of scented spike-flowers on the top terrace of the Pleasure House to wonder why he thought of serpents. He understood. Mankind's age-old hatred, brought from his native planet to the distant stars, was evil symbolized by a coil in a twisted, belly-path across the ground. And on Nahuatl, as well as a dozen other worlds, Wass was the serpent.

A night wind was rising, stirring the exotic, half-dozen other worlds' foliage planted cunningly on the terrace to simulate the mystery of an off-world jungle.

"Hume?" The inquiry seemed to come out of thin air over his head.

"Hume," he repeated his own name calmly.

A shaft of light brilliant enough to dazzle the eyes struck through the massed vegetation, revealing a path. Hume lingered for a moment, offering a counterstroke of indifference in what he had always known would be a test of wits. Wass was Veep of a shadowy empire, but that was apart from the world in which Ras Hume moved.

He strode deliberately down the corridor illuminated between leaf and blossom walls. A grotesque lump of crystal leered at him from the heart of a tharsala lilly bed. The intricate carving of a devilish nonhuman set of features was a work of alien art. Tendrils of smoke curled from the thing's flat nostrils, and Hume sniffed the scent of a narcotic he recognized. He smiled. Such measures might soften up the usual civ Wass interviewed here. But a star pilot turned out-hunter was immunized against such mind clouding.

There was a door, the lintel and posts of which had more carving, but this time Terran, Hume thought—old, very old. Perhaps rumor was right, Milfors Wass might be truly native Terran and not second, third, nor fourth generation star stock as most of those who reached Nahuatl were.

The room beyond that elaborately carved entrance was, in contrast, severe. Rust walls were bare of any pattern save an oval disk of cloudy golden shimmer behind the chair at the long table of solid ruby rock from Nahuatl's poisonous sister planet of Xipe. Without a pause he walked to the chair and seated himself without invitation to wait in the empty room.

That clouded oval might be a com device. Hume refused to look at it after his first glance. This interview was to be person to person. If Wass did not appear within a reasonable length of time he would leave.

And Hume hoped to any unseen watcher he presented the appearance of a man not impressed by stage settings. After all he was now in the seller's space boots, and it was a seller's market.

Ras Hume rested his right hand on the table. Against the polished glow of the stone, the substance of it was flesh-tanned brown—a perfect match for his left. And the subtle difference between true flesh and false was no hindrance in the use of those fingers or their strength. Save that it had pushed him out of command of a cargo-cum-liner and hurled him down from the pinnacle of a star pilot. There were bitter brackets about his mouth, set there by that hand as deeply as if carved with a knife.

It had been four years—planet time—since he had lifted the Rigal Rover from the launch pad on Sargon Two. He had suspected it might be a tricky voyage with young Tors Wazalitz, who was a third owner of the Kogan-Bors-Wazalitz line, and a Gratz chewer. But one did not argue with the owners, except when the safety of the ship was concerned. The Rigal Rover had made a crash landing at Alexbut, and a badly injured pilot had brought her in by will, hope and a faith he speedily lost.

He received a plasta-hand, the best the medical center could supply and a pension for life, forced by the public acclaim for a man who had saved ships and lives. Then— the sack because a crazed Tors Wazalitz was dead. They dared not try to stick Hume with a murder charge; the voyage record tapes had been shot straight through to the Patrol Council, and the evidence on those could be neither faked nor tampered with. They could not give him a quick punishment, but they could try to arrange a slow death. The word had gone out that Hume was off pilot boards. They had tried to keep him out of space.

And they might have done it, too, had he been the usual type of pilot, knowing only his trade. But some odd streak of restlessness had always led him to apply for the rim runs, the very first flights to newly opened worlds. Outside of the survey men, there were few qualified pilots of his seniority who possessed such a wide and varied knowledge of the galactic frontiers.

So when he learned that the ships' boards were irrevocably closed to him, Hume had signed up with the Out-Hunters' Guild. There was a vast difference between lifting a liner from a launching pad and guiding civ hunters to worlds surveyed and staked out for their trips into the wild. Hume relished the exploration part—he disliked the leading-by-the-hand of nine-tenths of the Guild's clients.

But if he had not been in the Guild service he would never have made that find on Jumala. That lucky, lucky find! Hume's plasta-flesh fingers curved, their nails drew across the red surface of the table. And where was Wass? He was about to rise and go when the golden oval on the wall smoked, its substance thinning to a mist as a man stepped through to the floor.

The newcomer was small compared to the former pilot, but he had breadth of shoulder which made the upper part of his torso overbalance his thin hips and legs. He was dressed most conservatively except for a jeweled plaque resting on the tightly stretched gray silk of his upper tunic at heart level. Unlike Hume he wore no visible arms belt, but the other did not doubt that there were a number of devices concealed in that room to counter the efforts of any assassin.

The man from the mirror spoke with a flat, toneless voice. His black hair had been shaven well above his ears, the locks left on top of his skull trained into a kind of bird's crest. As Hume, his visible areas of flesh were deeply browned, but by nature rather than exposure to space, the pilot guessed. His features were harsh, with a prominent nose, a back-slanting forehead, eyes dark, long and large, with heavy lids.

"Now—" He spread both his hands, palm down and flat on the table, a gesture Hume found himself for some unknown reason copying. "You have a proposition?"

But the pilot was not to be hurried, any more than he was to be influenced by Wass' stage-settings.

"I have an idea," he corrected.

"There are many ideas." Wass leaned back in his chair, but he did not remove his hands from the table. "Perhaps one in a thousand is the kernel of something useful. For the rest, there is no need to trouble a man."

"Agreed," Hume returned evenly. "But that one idea in a thousand can also pay off in odds of a million to one, when and if a man has it."

"And you have such a one?"

"I have such a one." It was Hume's role now to impress the other by his unshakable confidence. He had studied all the possibilities. Wass was the right man, perhaps the only partner he could find. But Wass must not know that.

"On Jumala?" Wass returned.

If that stare and statement was intended to rattle Hume it was a wasted shot. To discover that he had just returned from that frontier planet required no ingenuity on the Veep's part.

"Perhaps."

"Come, Out-Hunter Hume. We are both busy men, this is no time to play tricks with words and hints. Either you have made a find worth the attention of my organization or you have not. Let me be the judge."

This was it—the corner of no return. But Wass had his own code. The Veep had established his tight control of his lawless organization by set rules, and one of them was, don't be greedy. Wass was never greedy, which is why the patrol had never been able to pull him down, and those who dealt with him did not talk. If you had a good thing, and Wass accepted temporary partnership, he kept his side of the bargain rigidly. You did the same—or regretted your stupidity.

"A claimant to the Kogan estate—that good enough for you?"

Wass showed no surprise. "And how would such a claimant be profitable to us?"

Hume appreciated that "us"; he had an in now. "If you supply the claimant, surely you can claim a reward, in more ways than one."

"True. But one does not produce a claimant out of a Krusha dream. The investigation for any such claim now would be made by a verity lab and no imposture will pass those tests. While a real claimant would not need your help or mine."

"Depends upon the claimant."

"One you discovered on Jumala?"

"No." Hume shook his head slowly. "I found something else on Jumala—an L-B from Largo Drift intact and in good shape. From the evidence now in existence it could have landed there with survivors aboard."

"And the evidence of such survivors living on—that exists also?"

Hume shrugged, his plasta-flesh fingers flexed slightly. "It has been six planet years, there is a forest where the L-B rests. No, no evidence at present."

"The Largo Drift," Wass repeated slowly, "carrying, among others, Gentlefem Tharlee Kogan Brodie."

"And her son Rynch Brodie, who was at the time of the Largo Drift's disappearance a boy of fourteen."

"You have indeed made a find." Wass gave that simple statement enough emphasis to assure Hume he had won. His one-in-a-thousand idea had been absorbed, was now being examined, amplified, broken down into details he could never have hoped to manage for himself, by the most cunning criminal brain in at least five solar systems.

"Is there any hope of survivors?" Wass attacked the problem straight on.

"No evidence even of there being any passengers when the L-B planeted. Those are automatic and released a certain number of seconds after an accident alarm. For what it's worth the hatch of this one was open. It could have brought in survivors. But I was on Jumala for three months with a full Guild crew and we found no sign of any castaways."

"So you propose—?"

"On the basis of my report Jumala has been put up for a safari choice. The L-B could well be innocently discovered by a client. Every one knows the story with the case dragging through the Ten Sector-Terran Courts now. Gentlefem Brodie and her son might not have been news ten years ago. Now, with a third of the Kogan-Bors-Wazalitz control going to them, any find linked with the Largo Drift would gain full galactic coverage."

"You have a choice of survivor? The Gentlefem?"

Hume shook his head. "The boy. He was bright, according to the stories since, and he would have the survival manual from the ship to study. He could have grown up in the wilds of an unopened planet. To use a woman is too tricky."

"You are entirely right. But we shall require an extremely clever imposter."

"I think not." Hume's cool glance met Wass'. "We only need a youth of the proper general physical description and the use of a conditioner."

Wass' expression did not change, there was no sign that Hume's hint had struck home. But when he replied there was a slight change in the monotone of his voice.

"You seem to know a great deal."

"I am a man who listens," Hume replied, "and I do not always discount rumor as mere fantasy."

"That is true. As one of the guild you would be interested in the root of fact beneath the plant of fiction," Wass acknowledged. "You appear to have done some planning on your own."

"I have waited and watched for just such an opportunity as this," Hume answered.

"Ah, yes. The Kogan-Bors-Wazalitz combine incurred your displeasure. I see you are also a man who does not forget easily. And that, too, I understand. It is a foible of my own, Out-Hunter. I neither forget nor forgive my enemies, though I may seem to do so and time separates them from their past deeds for a space."

Hume accepted that warning—both must keep any bargain. Wass was silent for a moment, as if to leave time for the thought to root itself, then he spoke again.

"A youth with the proper physical qualifications. Have you any such in mind?"

"I think so." Hume was short.

"He will need certain memories; those take time to tape."

"Those dealing with Jumala, I can supply."

"Yes. You will have to provide a tape beginning with his arrival on that world. For such family material as is necessary I shall have ready. An interesting project, even apart from its value to us. This is one to intrigue experts."

Expert psycho-techs—Wass had them. Men who had slipped over the border of the law, had entered Wass' organization and prospered there. There were some techs crooked enough to enjoy such a project for its own sake, indulging in forbidden experimentation. For a moment, but only for a moment, something in Hume jibbed at the intent of carrying through his plan. Then he shrugged that tinge aside.

"How soon do you wish to move?"

"How long will preparation take?" Hume asked in return, for the second time battling a taste of concern.

"Three months, maybe four. There's research to be done and tapes to be made."

"It will be six months probably before the Guild sets up a safari for Jumala."

Wass smiled. "That need not worry us. When the time comes for a safari, there shall also be clients, impeccable clients, asking for it to be planned."

There would be, too, Hume knew. Wass' influence reached into places where the Veep himself was totally unknown. Yes, he could count on an excellent, well above suspicion, set of clients to discover Rynch Brodie when the time came.

"I can deliver the boy tonight, or early tomorrow morning. Where?"

"You are sure of your selection?"

"He fulfills the requirements, the right age, general appearance. A boy who will not be missed, who has no kin, no ties, and who will drop out of sight without any questions to be asked."

"Very well. Get him at once. Deliver him here."

Wass swept one hand across the table surface. On the red of the stone there glowed for seconds an address. Hume noted it, nodded. It was one in the center of the port town, one which could be visited at an odd hour without exciting any curiosity. He rose.

"He will be there."

"Tomorrow, at your convenience," Wass added, "you will come to this place." Again the palm moved and a second address showed on the table.

"There you will begin your tape for our use. It may take several sessions."

"I'm ready. I still have the long report to make to the Guild, so the material is still available on my note tapes."

"Excellent. Out-Hunter Hume, I salute a new colleague." At last Wass' right hand came up from the table. "May we both have luck equal to our industry."

"Luck to equal our desires," Hume corrected him.

"A very telling phrase, Out-Hunter. Luck to equal our desires. Yes, let us both deserve that."

CHAPTER TWO

The Starfall was a long way down scale from the pleasure houses of the upper town. Here strange vices were also merchandise, but not such exotics as Wass provided. This was strictly for crewmen of the star freighters who could be speedily and expertly separated from a voyage's pay in an evening. The tantalizing scents of Wass' terraces were reduced here to simply smells, the majority of which were not fragrant.

There had already been two fatal duels that evening. A tubeman from a rim ship had challenged a space miner to settle a difference with those vicious whips made from the tail casings of Flangoid flying lizards, an encounter which left both men in ribbons, one dead, one dying. And a scarred, ex-space marine had blaster-flamed one of the Star-and-Comet dealers into charred human ash.

The young man who had been ordered to help clear away the second loser retired to the stinking alley outside to lose the meal which was part of his meager day's pay. Now he crawled back inside, his face greenish, one hand pressed to his middle section.

He was thin, the fine bones of his face tight under the pallid skin, his ribs showing even through the sleazy fabric of the threadbare tunic with its house seal. When he leaned his head back against the grime encrusted wall, raising his face to the light, his hair had the glint of bright chestnut, a gold which was also red. And for his swamper's labor he was almost fastidiously clean.

"You—Lansor!"

He shivered as if an icy wind had found him and opened his eyes. They seemed disproportionately large in his skin and bone face and were of an odd shade, neither green nor blue, but somewhere between.

"Get going, you! Ain't paying out good credits for you to sit there like you was buying on your own!" The Salarkian who loomed above him spoke accentless, idiomatic Basic Space which came strangely from between his yellow lips. A furred hand thrust the handle of a mop-up stick at the young man, a taloned thumb jerked the direction in which to use that evil-smelling object. Vye Lansor levered himself up the wall, took the mop, setting his teeth grimly.

Someone had spilled a mug of Kardo and the deep purple liquid was already patterning the con-stone floor past any hope of cleaning. But he set to work slapping the fringe of the noisome mop back and forth to sop up what he could. The smell of the Kardo uniting with the general effluvia of the room and its inhabitants heightened his queasiness.

Working blindly in a half stupor, he was not aware of the man sitting alone in the booth until his mop spattered the ankle of one of the drinking girls. She struck him sharply across the face with a sputtering curse in the tongue of Altar-Ishtar.

The blow sent him back against the open lattice of the booth. As he tried to steady himself another hand reached up, fingers tightened about his wrist. He flinched, tried to jerk away from that hold, only to discover that he was the other's prisoner.

And looking down at his captor in apprehension, he was aware even then of the different quality of this man. The patron wore the tunic of a crewman, lighter patches where the ship's badges should have been to show that he was not engaged. But, though his tunic was shabby, dirty, his magnetic boots scuffed and badly worn, he was not like the others now enjoying the pleasures of the Starfall.

"This one—he makes trouble?" The vast bulk of the Vorm-man who was the Starfall's private law moved through the crowd with serene confidence in his own strength, which no one there, unless blind, deaf, and out-of-the-senses drunk, could dispute. His scaled, six-fingered, claw hand reached out for Lansor and the boy cringed.

"No trouble!" There was the click of authority in the voice of the man in the booth. His face, moments earlier taut and sharp with intelligence, was suddenly slack, his tone slurred as he answered: "Looks like an old shipmate. No trouble, just want a drink with an old shipmate."

But the grip which had pulled Vye forward, swung him around and down on the other bench in the booth, was anything but slack. The Vorm-man glanced from the patron of the Starfall to its least important employee and then grinned, thrusting his fanged jaws close to Lansor's.

"If the master wants to drink, you dirt-rat, you drink!"

Vye nodded vigorously, and then put his hand to his mouth, afraid his stomach was about to betray him again. Apprehensive, he watched the Vorm-man turn away. Only when that broad, green-gray back was lost in the smoky far reaches of the room did he expel his breath again.

"Here—" The grip was gone from his wrist, but fingers now put a mug into his hand. "Drink!"

He tried to protest, knew it was hopeless, and used both hands to get the mug to his lips, mouthing the stinging liquid in dull despair. Only, instead of bringing nausea with it, the stuff settled his stomach, cleared his head, with an after glow with which he managed to relax from the tense state of endurance which filled his hours in the Starfall.

Half of the mug's contents inside him and he dared to raise his eyes to the man opposite him. Yes, this was no common crewman, nor was he drunk as he had pretended for the Vorm-man. Now he watched the milling crowd with a kind of detachment, though Vye was sure he was aware of every move he himself made.

Vye finished the liquid. For the first time since he had come into this place two months earlier he felt like a real person again. And he had wits enough to guess that the potion he had just swallowed contained some drug. Only now he did not care at all. Anything which could wipe out in moments all the shame, fear, and sick despair the Starfall had planted in him was worth swallowing. Why the other had drugged him was a mystery, but he was content to wait for enlightenment.

Lansor's companion once more applied that compelling pressure to the younger man's bony forearm. Linked by that hold they left the Starfall, came into the cooler, far more pleasant atmosphere of the street. They were a block away before Vye's guide halted, though he did not release his prisoner.

"Forty names of Dugor!" he spat.

Lansor waited, breathing in the air of early morning. The confidence of the drug still held. At the moment he was certain nothing could be as bad as the life behind him, he was willing to face what this strange patron of the Starfall had in mind.

The other slapped his hand down on an air-car call button, stood waiting until one of the city flitters landed on beam before them.

From the seat of the air-car Vye noted they were heading into the respectability of the upper city, away from the stews ringing the launch port. He tried to guess their destination or purpose, not that either mattered much. Then the car descended on a landing stage.

The stranger waved Lansor through a doorway, down a short corridor into a room of private quarters. Vye sat down gingerly on the foam seat extending from the wall as he neared. He stared about. Dimly he could just remember rooms which had this degree of comfort, but so dimly now he could not be sure they did not exist only in his vivid imagination. For Vye's imagination had buoyed him first through the drab existence in a State Child's Crèche, then through a state-found job which he had lost because he could not adapt to the mechanical life of a computer tender, and had been an anchor and an escape when he had sunk through the depths of the port to the last refuge in the Starfall.

Now he pressed both his hands into the soft stuff of the seat and gaped at a small tri-dee on the wall facing him, a miniature scene of life on some other planet wherein a creature enveloped in short black and white striped fur crept belly flat, to stalk long-legged, short-winged birds making blood-red splotches against yellow reed banks under a pale violet sky. He feasted on its color, on the sense of freedom and off-world wonders which it raised in him.

"Who are you?"

The stranger's abrupt question brought him back, not only to the room but to his own precarious position. He moistened his lips, no longer quite so aglow with confidence.

"Vye—Vye Lansor." Then he added his other identification, "S. C. C. 425061."

"State child, eh?" The other had pushed a button for a refresher cup, then was sipping its contents slowly. He did not ring for a second to offer Vye. "Parents?"

Lansor shook his head. "I was brought in after the Five-Hour Fever epidemic. They didn't try to keep records, there were too many of us."

The man was watching him levelly over the rim of that cup. There was something cold in that study, something which curbed Vye's pleasant feeling of only moments earlier. Now the other set down his drink, crossed the room. Cupping his hand under Lansor's chin, he brought up his head in a way which stirred a sullen resentment in the younger man, yet something told him resistance would only bring trouble.

"I'd say Terran stock—not more than second generation." He was talking to himself more than to Vye. He loosed his hold on the boy's chin, but he still stood there surveying him from head to foot. Lansor wanted to squirm, but he fought that impulse, and managed to meet the other's gaze when it reached his face again.

"No—not the usual port-drift. I was right all the way." Now he looked at Vye again as if the younger man did have a brain, emotions, some call on his interest as a personality. "Want a job?"

Lansor pressed his hand deeper into the foam seat. "What—what kind?" He was angry and ashamed at that small betraying break in his voice.

"You have scruples?" The stranger appeared to think that amusing. Vye reddened, but he was also more than a little surprised that the man in the worn space uniform had read hesitancy right. Someone out of the Starfall should not be too particular about employment, and he could not tell why he was.

"Nothing illegal, I assure you." The man crossed to set his refresher cup in the empty slot. "I am an Out-Hunter."

Lansor blinked. This had all taken on some of the fantastic aura of a dream. The other was eyeing him impatiently, as if he had expected some reaction.

"You may inspect my credentials if you wish."

"I believe you," Vye found his voice.

"I happen to need a gearman."

But this wasn't happening! Of course, it couldn't happen to him, Vye Lansor, state child, swamper in the Starfall. Things such as this did not happen, except in a thaline dream, and he wasn't a smoke eater! It was the kind of dream a man didn't want to wake from, not if he was port-drift.

"Would you be willing to sign on?"

Vye tried to clutch reality to himself, to remain level-headed. A gearman for an Out-Hunter! Why five men out of six would pay a large premium for a chance at such rating. The chill of doubt cut through the first hazy rosiness. A swamper from a port-side dive simply did not become a gearman for a Guild Hunter.

Again it was as if the stranger read his thoughts. "Look here," he spoke abruptly. "I had a bad time myself, years ago. You resemble someone to whom I owe a debt. I can't repay him, but I can make the scales a little even this way."

"Make the scales even." Vye's fading hope brightened. Then the Out-Hunter was a follower of the Fata Rite. That would explain everything. If you could not repay a good deed to the one you owed, you must balance the Eternal Scales in another fashion. He relaxed again, a great many of his unasked questions so answered.

"You will accept?"

Vye nodded eagerly. "Yes, Out-Hunter." He still could not believe that this was happening.

The other pressed the refresher button, and this time he handed Lansor the brimming cup. "Drink on the bargain." His words had the ring of command.

Lansor drank, gulping down the contents of the cup, and suddenly was aware of being tired. He leaned back against the wall, his eyes closed.

Ras Hume took the cup from the lax fingers of the young man. So far, very good. Chance appeared to be playing on his side of the board. It had been chance which had steered him into the Starfall just three nights ago when he had been in quest of his imposter. And Vye Lansor was better than he dared hope to find. The boy had the right coloring, he had been batted around enough to fall for the initial story, he was malleable now. And after Wass' techs worked on him he would be Rynch Brodie—heir to one-third of Kogan-Bors-Wazalitz!

"Come!" He touched Vye on the shoulder. The boy opened his eyes but his gaze did not focus as he got slowly to his feet. Hume glanced at his planet-time watch. It was still very early; the chance he must run in getting Lansor out of this building was small if they went at once. Guiding the younger man with a light hold above the elbow, he walked him out back to the flitter landing stage. The air-car was waiting. Hume's sense of being a gambler facing a run of good luck grew as he shepherded the boy into the flitter, punched a cover destination and took off.

On another street he transferred himself and his charge into a second air-car, set the destination to within a block of the address Wass had given him. Not much later he walked Vye into a small lobby with a discreet list of names posted in its rack. No occupations attached to those colored streamers Hume noted. This meant either that their owners represented luxury trades, where a name signified the profession or service, or that they were covers—perhaps both. Wass' world fringed many different circles, intermingled with some quite surprising professions dedicated to the comfort, pleasure or health of the idle rich, off-world nobility, and the criminal elite.

Hume fingered the right call button, knowing that the thumb pattern he had left on Wass' conference table would have already been relayed as his symbol of admission here. A flicker of light winked below the name, the wall to the right shimmered, and produced a doorway. Steering Vye to it, Hume nodded to the man waiting there. He was a flat-faced Eucorian of the servant caste, and now he reached out to draw Lansor over the threshold.

"I have him, gentlehomo." His voice was as expressionless as his face. There was another shimmer and the door disappeared.

Hume brushed his hand down the outer side of his thigh, wiping flesh against the coarse stuff of the crew uniform. He left the lobby frowning at his own thoughts.

Stupid! A swamper from one of the worst rat holes in the port. Like as not that youngster would have had his brains kicked out in a brawl, or been fried to a crisp when some drunk got wild with a blaster, before the year was out. He'd done him a real kindness, given him a chance at a future less than one man in a billion ever had the power to even dream about. Why, if Vye Lansor had known what was going to happen to him, he would have been so willing to volunteer, that he would have dragged Hume here. There was no reason to have any regrets over the boy, he had never had it so good—never! There was only one small period of risk for Vye to face. Those days he would have to spend alone on Jumala between the time Wass' organization would plant him there and the coming of Hume's party to "discover" him. Hume himself would tape every possible aid to cover that period. All the knowledge of a Guild Out-Hunter, added to the information gathered by the survey, would be used to provide Rynch Brodie with the training necessary for wilderness survival. Hume was already listing the items to be included as he strode down the street, his tread once more assured.

CHAPTER THREE

His head ached dully, of that he was conscious first. As he turned, without opening his eyes, he felt the brush of softness against his cheek, and a pungent odor fill his nostrils.

He opened his eyes, stared up past a rim of broken rock toward the cloudless, blue-green sky. A relay clicked into proper place deep in his mind.

Of course! He had been trying to lure a strong-jaws out of its traphole with hooked bait, then his foot had slipped. Rynch Brodie sat up, flexed his bare thin arms, and moved his long legs experimentally. No broken bones, anyway. But still he frowned. Odd—that dream which jarred with the here and now.

Crawling to the side of the creek, he dipped head and shoulders into the water, letting the chill of the stream flush away some of his waking bewilderment. He shook himself, making the drops fly from his uncovered torso and arms, and then discovered his hunting tackle.

He stood for a moment fingering each piece of his scanty clothing, recalling every piece of labor or battle which had added pouch, belt, strip of fabric to his equipment. Yet—there was still that odd sense of strangeness, as if none of this was really his.

Rynch shook his head, wiped his wet face with his arm. It was all his, that was sure, every bit of it. He'd been lucky, the survival manual on the L-B had furnished him with general directions and this was a world which was not unfriendly—not if one was prepared for trouble.

He climbed up and loosened the net, coiling its folds into one hand, taking the good spear in his other. A bush stirred ahead, against the pull of the light breeze. Rynch froze, then the haft of his spear slid into a new hand grip, the coils of his net spun out. A snarl cut over the purr of water.

The scarlet blot which sprang for his throat was met with the flail of the net. Rynch stabbed twice at the creature he had so swept off balance. A water-cat, this year's cub. Dying, its claws, over-long in proportion to its paws, drew inch deep furrows in the earth and gravel. Its eyes, almost the same shade as its long, burr-entangled body fur, glared up at him in deathly enmity.

As Rynch watched, that feeling that he was studying something strange, utterly alien, came to him once again. Yet he had hunted water-cats for many seasons. Fortunately they were solitary, evil-tempered beasts that marked out a roaming territory to defend it from others of their kind, and not too many were to be encountered in cross-country travel.

He stooped to pull his net from the now still paws. Some definite place he must reach. The compulsion to move on in that sudden flash shook him, raised the dull ache still troubling his temples into a punishing throb. Going down on his knees, Rynch once more turned to the stream water; this time after splashing it onto his face, he drank from his cupped hands.

Rynch swayed, his wet hands over his eyes, digging fingertips into the skin of his forehead to ease that pain bursting in his skull. Sitting in a room, drinking from a cup—it was as if a shadow picture fitted over the reality of the stream, rocks and brush about him. He had sat in a room, had drank from a cup—that action had been important!

A sharp, hot pain made him lose contact with that shadow. He looked down. From the gravel, from under rocks, gathered an army of blue-black, hard-shelled things, their clawed forelimbs extended, blue sense organs raised on fleshy stalks well above their heads, all turned towards the dead feline.

Rynch slapped out vigorously, stumbled into the water loosening the hold of two vicious scavengers on the torn skin of his ankle when he waded out knee-deep. Already that black tongue of small bodies licked across the red-haired side of the hunter. Within minutes the corpse would be only well-cleaned bones.

Retrieving his spear and net, Rynch immersed both in the water to clean off attackers, and hurried on, splashing through the creek until he was well away from the vicinity of the kill. A little later he flushed a four-footed creature from between two rocks and killed it with one blow from his spear haft. He skinned his kill, feeling the substance of the skill. Was it exceedingly rough hide, or rudimentary scales? And knew a return of that puzzlement.

He felt, he thought painfully as he toasted the dry looking, grayish meat on a sharpened stick, as if a part of him knew very well what manner of animal he had killed. And yet, far inside him, another person he could not understand stood aloof watching in amazement.

He was Rynch Brodie, and he had been traveling on the Largo Drift with his mother.

Memory presented him automatically with a picture of a thin woman with a narrow, rather unhappy face, a twist of elaborately dressed hair in which jeweled lights sparkled. There had been something bad—memory was no longer exact but chaotic. And his head ached as he tried to recall that time with greater clarity. Afterwards the L-B and a man with him in it—

"Simmons Tait!"

An officer, badly hurt. He had died when the L-B landed here. Rynch had a clear memory of himself piling rocks over Tait's twisted body. He had been alone then with only the survival manual and some of the L-B supplies. The important thing was that he must never forget he was Rynch Brodie.

He licked grease from his fingers. The ache in his head made him drowsy. He curled up on a patch of sun-warmed sand and slept.

Or did he? His eyes were open again. Now the sky above him was no longer a bowl of light, but rather a muted halo of evening. Rynch sat up, his heart pounding as if he had been racing to outdistance the rising wind now pushing against his half-naked body.

What was he doing here? Where *was* here?

Panic, carried through from that awakening, dried his mouth, roughened his skin, made wet the palms of the hands he dug into the sand on either side of him. Vaguely, a picture projected into his mind—he had sat in a room, and watched a man come to him with a cup. Before that, he had been in a place of garish light and evil smells.

But he was Rynch Brodie, he had come here on an L-B when he was a boy, he had buried the ship's officer under a pile of rocks, managed to survive by himself because he had applied the aids in the boat to learn how. This morning he had been hunting a strong-jaw, tempting it out of its hiding by a hook and line and a bait of fresh killed skipper.

Rynch's hands went to his face, he crouched forward on his knees. That all was true, he could prove it—he would prove it! There was the strong-jaw's den back there, somewhere on the rise where he had left the snapped haft of the spear he had broken in his fall. If he could find the den, then he would be sure of the reality of everything else.

He had only had a very real dream—that was it! Only, why did he continue to dream of that room, that man, and the cup? Of the place of lights and smells, which he hated so much that the hate was a sour taste in his fright-dried mouth? None of it had ever been a part of Rynch Brodie's world.

Through the dusk he started back up the stream bed, towards the narrow little valley where he had wakened after that fall. Finally, finding shelter within the heart of a bush, he crouched low, listening to the noises of another world which awoke at night to take over the stage from the day dwellers.

As he plodded back, he fought off panic, realizing that some of those noises he could identify with confidence, while others remained mysteries. He bit down hard on the knuckles of his clenched fist, attempting to bend that discovery into evidence. Why did he know at once that that thin, eerie wailing was the flock call of a leather-winged, feathered tree dweller, and that a coughing grunt from downstream was just a noise?

"Rynch Brodie—Largo Drift—Tait." He tasted the blood his teeth drew from his own skin as he recited that formula. Then he scrambled up. His feet tangled in the net, and he went down again, his head cracking on a protruding root.

Nothing tangible reached him in that brush shelter. What did venture out of hiding to investigate was a substance none of his species could have named. It was neither body, nor mind—perhaps it was closest to alien emotion.

Making contact stealthily, but with confidence, it explored after its own fashion. Then, puzzled, it withdrew to report. And since that to which it reported was governed by a set pattern which had not been altered for eons, its only answer was a basic command reaffirmed. Again it made contact, strove to carry out that order fruitlessly. Where it should have found easy passage, a clear channel to carry influence to the sleeper's brain, it found a jumble of impressions, interwoven until they made a protective barrier.

The invader strove to find some pattern, or meaning— withdrew baffled. But its invasion, as ghostly as that had been, loosened a knot here, cleared a passage there.

Rynch awoke at dawn, slowly, dazedly, sorting out sounds, smells, thoughts. There was a room, a man, trouble and fear, then there was he, Rynch Brodie, who had lived in this wilderness on an unmapped frontier world for the passage of many seasons. That world was about him now, he could feel its winds, hear its sounds, taste, smell. It was not a dream—the other was the dream. It had to be!

Prove it. Find the L-B, retrace the trail of yesterday past the point of the fall which had started all this. Right there was the slope down which he must have tumbled. Above, he would find the den he had been exploring when the accident had occurred.

Only—he did not find it. His mind had produced a detailed picture of that rounded depression, at the bottom of which the strong-jaw lurked. But when he reached the crown of the bluff, nowhere did he sight the mounded earth of the pit's rim. He searched carefully for a good length, both north and south. No den—no trace of one.

Yet his memory told him that there had been one here yesterday.

Had he fallen elsewhere and stumbled on, dazed, to fall a second time?

Some disputant inside him said no to that. This was where he had regained consciousness yesterday and there was no den!

He faced away from the river, breathing fast. No den—was there also no L-B? If he had passed this way dazed from a former fall, surely he would have left some trace.

There was a crushed, browned plant flattened by weight. He stooped to finger the wilted leaves. Something had come in this direction. He would back-track. Rynch gave a hunter's attention to the ground.

A half-hour later he found nothing but some odd, almost obliterated marks on grass too resilient to hold traces very long. And from them he could make nothing.

He knew where he was, even if he did not know how he got here. The L-B—if it did exist—was to the west. He had a vivid mental picture of the rocket shape, its once silvery sides dulled by exposure, canted crookedly amid trees. And he was going to find it!

Beyond the edge of any conscious sense there was a new stir. He was contacted again, tested. A forest called delicately in its alien way. Rynch had a fleeting thought of trees, was not aware of more than a mild desire to see what lay in their shade.

For the present his own problem held him. That which beckoned was defeated, repulsed by his indifference. While Rynch started at a steady distance to trot towards the east, far away a process akin to a relay clicked into a second set of impulse orders.

Well above the planet Hume spun a dial to bring in the image of the wide stretches of continents, the small patches of seas. They would set down on the western land mass. Its climate, geographical features and surface provided the best site. And he had the very important co-ordinates for their camp already taped in the directo.

"That's Jumala."

He did not glance around to see what effect that screen view had on the other four men in the control cabin of the safari ship. Just now he was striving to master his impatience. The slightest hint could give birth to a suspicion which would blast their whole scheme. Wass might have had a hand in the selection of the three clients, but they would certainly be far from briefed on the truth of any discovery made on Jumala—they had to be for the safety of the whole enterprise.

The fourth man, serving as his gearman for this trip, was Wass' own insurance against any wrong move on Hume's part. And the Out-Hunter respected him as being man enough to be wary of giving any suspicion of going counter to the agreed plan.

Dawn was touching up the main points of the western continent, and he must set this spacer down within a day's journey of the abandoned L-B. Exploration in that direction would be the first logical move for his party. They could not be openly steered to the find, but there were ways of directing a hunt which would do as well.

Two days ago, according to schedule, their castaway had been deposited here with a sub-conscious command to remain in the general area. There had been a slight element of risk in leaving him alone, armed only with the crude weapons he could manipulate, but that was part of the gamble.

They were down—right on the mark. Hume saw to the unpacking and activating of those machines and appliances which would protect and serve his civ clients. He slapped the last inflate valve on a bubble tent, watched it critically as it billowed from a small roll of fabric into a weather resistant, one-room, air-conditioned and heated shelter.

"Ready and waiting for you to move in, Gentlehomo," he reported to the small man who stood gazing about him with a child's wondering interest in the new and strange.

"Very ingenious, Hunter. Ah—now just what might that be?" His voice was also eager as he pointed a finger to the east.

CHAPTER FOUR

Hume glanced up alertly. There was a bare chance that "Brodie" might have witnessed their arrival and might be coming in now to save them all a great amount of time and trouble by acting the overjoyed, rescued castaway.

But he could sight nothing at all in that direction to excite any attention. The distant mountains provided a stark, dark blue background. Up their foothills and lower slopes was a thick furring of trees with foliage of so deep a green as to register black from this distance. And on the level country was the lighter blue-green of the other variety of wood edging the open country about the river. In there rested the L-B.

"I don't see anything!" he snapped, so sharply the little man stared at him in open surprise. Hume forced a quick smile.

"Just what did you sight, Gentlehomo Starns? There is no large game in the woodlands."

"This was not an animal, Hunter. Rather a flash of light, just about there." Again he pointed.

Sun, Hume thought, could have been reflected from some portion of the L-B. He had believed that small spacer so covered with vines and ringed in by trees that it could not have been so sighted. But a storm might have disposed of some of nature's cloaking. If so Starns' interest must be fed, he would make an ideal discoverer.

"Odd." Hume produced his distance glasses. "Just where, Gentlehomo?"

"There." Starns obligingly pointed a third time.

If there had been anything to see it was gone now. But it did lie in the right direction. For a second or two Hume was uneasy. Things seemed to be working too well; his cynical distrust was triggered by fitting so smoothly.

"Might be the sun," he observed.

"Reflected from some object you mean, Hunter? But the flash was very bright. And there could be no mirror surface in there, surely there could not be?"

Yes, things were moving too fast. Hume might be overly cautious but he was determined that no hint of any pre-knowledge of the L-B must ever come to these civs. When they would find the Largo Drift's life boat and locate Brodie, there would be a legal snarl. The castaway's identity would be challenged by a half dozen distant and unloving relatives, and there would be an intense inquiry. These civs must be the impartial witnesses.

"No, I hardly believe in a mirror in an uninhabited forest, Gentlehomo," he chuckled. "But we are on a hunting planet and not all its life forms have yet been classified."

"You are thinking of an intelligent native race, Hunter?" Chambriss, the most demanding of the civ party, strode up to join them.

Hume shook his head. "No native intelligence on a hunting world, Gentlehomo. That is assured before the planet is listed for a safari. However, a bird or flying thing, perhaps with metallic plumage or scales to catch the sunlight, might under the right circumstances seem a flash of light. That has happened before."

"It was *very* bright," Starns said doubtfully. "We might look over there later."

"Nonsense!" Chambriss spoke briskly as one used to overriding the conflicting wishes in any company. "I came here for a water-cat, and a water-cat I'm going to have. You don't find those in wooded areas."

"There will be a schedule," Hume announced. "Each of you has signed up, according to contract, for a different trophy. You for a water-cat, Gentlehomo. And you, Gentlehomo Starns, want to make tri-dees of the pit-dragons. While Gentlehomo Yactisi wishes to try electo fishing in the deep holes. To alternate days is the fair way. And, who knows, each of you may discover your own choice near the other man's stake out."

"You are quite right, Hunter," Starns nodded. "And since my two colleagues have chosen to try for a water creature, perhaps we should start along the river."

It was two days, then, before they could work their way into the woods. One part of Hume protested, the more cautious section of his mind was appeased. He saw, beyond the three clients now turning over and sorting space bags, Wass' man glanced at the woods and then back to Starns. And, being acutely aware of all undercurrents here, Hume wondered what the small civ had actually seen.

The camp was complete, a cluster of seven bubble tents not too far from the ship. At least this crowd did not appear to consider that the Hunter was there to do all the serious moving and storing of supplies. All three of the clients pitched in to help, and Wass' man went down to the river to return with half a dozen silver-fins cleaned and threaded on a reed, ready to broil over the cook unit.

A fire in the night was not needed except to afford the proper stage setting. But it was enjoyed. Hume leaned forward to feed the flames, and Starns pushed some lengths of driftwood closer.

"You have said, Hunter, that hunting worlds never contain intelligent native life. Unless the planet is minutely explored how can your survey teams be sure of that fact?" His voice bordered on the pedantic, but his interest was plain.

"By using the verifier." Hume sat crosslegged, his plasta-hand resting on one knee. "Fifty years ago, we would have had to keep rather a lengthy watch to be sure of a free world. Now, we plant verifiers at suitable test points. Intelligence means mental activity of some sort— any of which would be recorded on the verifier."

"Amazing!" Starns extended his plump hands to the flames in the immemorial gesture of a human attracted not only to the warmth of the burning wood, but to its promise of security against the forces of the dark. "No matter how few, or how scattered your native thinkers may be, you record them without missing any?"

Hume shrugged. "Maybe one or two," he grinned, "might get through such a screening. But we have yet to discover a planet with such a sparse native life as that at the level of intelligence."

Yactisi juggled a cup in and out of the firelight. "I agree, this is most interesting." He was a thin man, with scanty drab gray hair and dark skin, perhaps the result of the mingling of several human races. His eyes were slightly sunken, so that it was difficult in this light to read their expression. He was, Hume had already decided, a class one brain and observant to a degree, which could either be a help or a menace. "There have been no cases of failure?"

"None reported," Hume returned. All his life he had relied on machines operating, of course, under the competent domination of men trained to use them properly. He understood the process of the verifier, had seen it at work. At the Guild Headquarters there were no records of its failure; he was willing to believe it was infallible.

"A race residing in the sea now—could you be sure your machine would discover its presence?" Starns continued to question.

Hume laughed. "Not to be found on Jumala, you may be sure of that—the seas here are small and shallow. Such, not to be picked up by the verifier, would have to exist at great depths and never venture on land. So we need not fear any surprises here. The Guild takes no chances."

"As it always continues to assure one," Yactisi replied. "The hour grows late. I wish you rewarding dreams." He arose to go to his own bubble tent.

"Yes, indeed!" Starns blinked at the fire and then scrambled up in turn. "We hunt along the river, then, tomorrow?"

"For water-cat," Hume agreed. Of the three, he believed Chambriss the most impatient. Might as well let him pot his trophy as soon as possible. The ex-pilot deduced there would be little cooperation in exploration from that client until he was satisfied in his own quest.

Rovald, Wass' man, lingered by the fire until the three civs were safe in their bubbles.

"River range tomorrow?" he asked.

"Yes. We can't rush the deal."

"Agreed." Rovald spoke with a curtness he did not use when the civs were present. "Only don't delay too long. Remember, our boy's roaming around out there. He might just be picked off by something before these stumble-footed civs catch up with him."

"That's the chance we knew we'd have to take. We don't dare raise any suspicion. Yactisi, for one, is no fool, neither is Starns. Chambriss just wants to get his water-cat, but he could become nasty if anyone tried to steer him."

"Too long a wait might run us into trouble. Wass doesn't like trouble."

Hume spun around. In the half light of the fire his features were set, his mouth grim. "Neither do I, Rovald, neither do I!" he said softly, but with an icy promise beneath the words.

Rovald was not to be intimidated. He grinned. "Set your fins down, fly-boy. You need Wass—and I'm here to hold his stakes for him. This is a big deal, we won't want any misses!"

"There won't be any—not from my side." Hume stepped away from the fire, approached a post which gleamed with a dull, red line of fire down either side. He pressed a control button. That red line flared into a streak of brilliance. Now encircling the bubble tents and the space ship was a force field: routine protection of a safari camp on a strange world and one Hume had set as a matter of course.

He stood for a long moment staring through that invisible barrier toward the direction of the wood. It was a dark night, there were scudding clouds to hide the stars, which meant rain probably before morning. This was no time to be plagued by uncertain weather.

Somewhere out there Brodie was holed up. He hoped the boy had long ago reached the "camp" so carefully erected and left for his occupancy. The L-B, that stone covered "grave" showing signs of several years' occupancy, was all assembled and constructed to the last small detail. Far less might have deceived the civs in this safari. But as soon as the story of their find leaked, there would be others on the scene, men trained to assess the signs of a castaway's fight for survival. His own Guild training and the ability of Wass' renegade techs should bring them through that test.

What had Starns seen? The glint of sun on the tail of the L-B, tilted now to the sky? Hume walked slowly back to the fire, when he saw Rovald going up the ramp into the spacer. He smiled. Did Wass think he was stupid enough not to guess that the Veep's man would be in com touch with his employer? Rovald was about to report along some channel of the shadow world that they had landed and that the play was about to begin. Hume wondered idly how far and through how many relays that message would pass before it reached its destination.

He stretched and yawned, moving to his sleeping pad. Tomorrow they must find Chambriss a water-cat. Hume shoved Brodie into the back of his mind to center his thoughts on the various ways of delivering, to the waiting sportsman, a fair-sized alien feline.

The lights in the bubbles went out one by one. Within the circle barrier of the force field men slept. And by midnight the rain began to fall, streaming down the sides of the bubbles, soaking the ashes of the fire.

Out of the dark crept that which was not thought, not substance, but alien to the off-world men. But the barrier, meant to deter multi-footed creatures, with wings or no visible limbs at all, proved to be a better protection than its creators had hoped. There was no penetration—only a baffled butting of one force against another. And then the probe withdrew as undetected as it had come.

Only, the thing which had no intelligence, as humankind rated intelligence, did possess the ability to fathom the nature of that artificial barrier. The force field was examined, its nature digested. First approach had failed.

The second was now ready—ready as it had not been months before when the first coming of these creatures had alerted the very ancient watchdog on Jumala.

Deep in the darker woods on the mountain sides there was a stirring. Things whimpered in their sleep, protested subconsciously commands they could never understand, only obey. With the coming of dawn there would be a marshaling of hosts, a new assault—not on the camp, but on any leaving its protection. And also on the boy now sleeping in a shallow cave formed by the swept roots of a tree—a tree which had crashed when the L-B landed.

Again, fortune favored Hume. With the dawn the rain was over. There was a cloudy sky overhead, but he believed the day would clear. The roily, rushing water of the river would aid Chambriss' quest. Water-cats holed up in the banks, but rising water often forced them out of such dens. A course parallel to the stream bed could well show them the tracks of one of the felines.

They started off in a group, Hume leading, with Chambriss treading briskly behind him, Rovald bringing up the rear in the approved trail technique. Chambriss carried a needler, Starns was unarmed except for a small protection stunner, his tri-dee box slung on his chest by well-worn carrying straps. Yactisi shouldered an electric pole, wore its control belt buckled about his middle, though Hume had warned him that the storm would prevent any deep hole fishing.

Only a short distance from the campsite they came upon the unmistakable marks of a water-cat's broad paws, pressed in so heavy and distinct a pattern that Hume knew the animal could not be far ahead. The indentations were deep, and he measured the distance between them with the length of his hand.

"Big one!" Chambriss exclaimed in satisfaction. "Going away from the river, too."

That point puzzled Hume slightly. The red coated felines might be washed out of their burrows, but they did not willingly head so sharply away from the water. He squatted on his heels and surveyed the stretch of countryside between them and the distant wood with care.

The grass was this season's, still growing, not tall enough to afford cover for an animal with paws as large as these prints. There were two clumps of brush. It could have holed up in either, waiting to attack any trailer—but why? It had not been wounded, nor frightened by their party, there was no reason for it to set an ambush on its back trail.

Starns and Yactisi dropped back, though Starns was fussing with his tri-dee. Rovald caught up. He had drawn his ray tube in answer to Hume's hand wave. Any action foreign to the regular habits of an animal was to be mistrusted.

Getting to his feet Hume paced along the line of marks. They were fresh—hot fresh. And they still led in a straight line for the woods. With another wave of his hand he stopped Chambriss. The civ was trained in spite of his eagerness and obeyed. Hume left the tracks, made a detour which brought him to a point from which he could study those clumps of brush. No sign except that line of prints pointed to the woods. And if the party kept on, they might well come upon the L-B!

He decided to risk it. But when they were less than a couple of yards from the tree fringe his hand shot up to direct Chambriss to fire towards the quivering bush.

Only, that formless half seen thing, hardly to be distinguished in color from the vegetation, was no water-cat. There was a thin, ragged cry. Then the creature plunged backward, was gone.

"What in the name of nine Gods was that?" Chambriss demanded.

"I don't know." Hume went forward, jerked the needler dart from a tree trunk. "But don't shoot again—not unless you are sure of what you are aiming at!"

CHAPTER FIVE

Moisture from the night's rain hung on the tree leaves, clung in globules to Rynch's sweating body. He lay on a wide branch trying to control the heavy panting which supplied his laboring lungs. And he could still hear the echoes of the startled cries which had come from the men who had threaded through the woods to the up-pointed tail fins of the L-B.

Now he tried to reason why he had run. They were his own kind, they would take him out of the loneliness of a world heretofore empty of his species. But that tall man—the one who had led the party into the irregular clearing about the life boat—

Rynch shivered, dug his nails into the wood on which he lay. At the sight of that man, dream and reality had crashed together, sending him into panic-stricken flight. That was the man from the room—the man with the cup!

As his heart quieted he began to think more coherently. First, he had not been able to find the strong-jaws's den. Then the marks on the ground at the point from which he had fallen and the L-B were here, just as he remembered. But not far from the small ship he had discovered something more—a campsite with a shelter fashioned out of spalls and vines, containing possessions a castaway might have accumulated.

That man would come, Rynch was sure of that, but he was too spent to struggle on.

No, the answer to every part of the puzzle lay with that man. To go back to the ship clearing was to risk capture—

but he had to know. Rynch looked with more attention at his present surroundings. Deep mold under the trees here would hold tracks. There might just be another way to move. He eyed the spread of limbs on a neighbor tree.

His journey through those heights was awkward and he sweated and cringed when he disturbed vocal treetop dwellers. He was also to discover that close to the site of the L-B crash others waited.

He huddled against the bole of a tree when he made out the curve of a round bulk holding tight to the tree trunk aloft. Though it was balled in upon itself he was sure the creature was fully as large as he, and the menacing claws suggested it was a formidable opponent.

When it made no move to follow him Rynch began to hope it had only been defending its own hiding place, for its present attitude suggested concealment.

Still facing that featureless blob in the tree, the man retreated, alert for the first sign of advance on the part of the creature above. None came, and he dared to slip around the bole of the tree under which he stood, listening intently for any corresponding movement overhead. Now he was facing that survivor's camp.

Another object crouched in the dark of the lean-to shelter, just as its fellow was on sentry duty in the tree! Only this one did not have the self-color of the foliage to disguise it. Four-limbed, its long forearms curved about its bent knees, its general outline almost that of a human—if a human went clothed in a thick fuzz. The head hunched right against the shoulders as if the neck were very short, or totally lacking, was pear-shaped, with the longer end to the back, and the sense organs of eyes and nose squeezed together on the lower quarter of the rounded portion, with a line of wide mouth to split the blunt round of the muzzle. Dark pits for eyes showed no pupil, iris, or cornea. The nose was a black, perfectly rounded tube jutting an inch or so beyond the cheek surface. Grotesque, alien and terrifying, it made no hostile move. And, since it had not turned its head, he could not be sure it had even sighted him. But it knew he was there, he was certain of that. And was waiting—for what? As the long seconds crawled by Rynch began to believe that it was not waiting for him. Heartened, he pulled at the vine loop, climbed back into the tree.

Minutes later he discovered that there were more than two of the beasts waiting quietly about the camp, and that their sentry line ran between him and the clearing of the L-B. He withdrew farther into the wood, intent upon finding a detour which would bring him out into the open lands. Now he wanted to join forces with his own kind, whether those men were potential enemies or not.

As time passed the beasts closed about the clearing of the camp. Afternoon was fading into evening when he reached a point several miles downstream near the river. Since he had come into the open he had not sighted any of the watchers. He hoped they did not willingly venture out of the trees where the leaves were their protection.

Rynch went flat on the stream bank, made a worm's progress up the slope to crouch behind a bush and survey the land immediately ahead. There stood an off-world spacer, fins down, nose skyward, and grouped not too far from its landing ramp, a collection of bubble tents. A fire burned in their midst and men were moving about it.

Now that he was free from the wood and its watchers and had come so near to his goal, Rynch was curiously reluctant to do the sensible thing, to rise out of concealment and walk up to that fire, to claim rescue by his own kind.

The man he sought stood by the fire, shrugging his arms into a webbing harness which brought a box against his chest. Having made that fast he picked up a needler by its sling. By their gestures the others were arguing with him, but he shook his head, came on, to be a shadow stalking among other shadows. One of the men trailed him, but as they reached a post planted a little beyond the bubble tents he stopped, allowed the explorer to advance alone into the dark.

Rynch went to cover under a bush. The man was heading to the stream bed. Had they somehow learned of his own presence nearby, were they out to find him? But the preparations the tall man had made seemed more suited to going on patrol. The watchers! Was the other out to spy on them? That idea made sense. And in the meantime he would let the other past him, follow along behind until he was far enough from the camp so that his friends could not interfere—then, they would have a meeting!

Rynch's fingers balled into fists. He would find out what was real, what was a dream in this crazy, mixed up mind of his! That other would know, and would tell him the truth!

Alert as he was, he lost sight of the stranger who melted into the dusky cover of the shadows. Then came a quiet ripple of water close to his own hiding place. The man from the spacer camp was using the stream as his road.

In spite of his caution Rynch was close to betrayal as he edged around a clump of vegetation growing half in, half out of the stream. Only a timely rustle told him that the other had sat down on a drift log.

Waiting for him? Rynch froze, so startled that he could not think clearly for a second. Then he noted that the outline of the other's body was visible, growing brighter by the moment.

Minute particles of pale-greenish radiance were gathering about the other. The dark shadow of an arm flapped, the radiance swirled, broke again into pinpoint sparks.

Rynch glanced down at his own body—the same sparks were drifting in about him, edging his arms, thighs, chest. He pushed back into the bushes while the sparks still flitted, but they no longer gathered in strength enough to light his presence. Now he could see they drifted about the vegetation, about the log where the man sat, about rocks and reeds. Only they were thicker about the stranger as if his body were a magnet. He continued to keep them whirling by means of waving hand and arm, but there was enough light to show Rynch the fingers of his other hand, busy on the front panel of the box he wore.

That fingering stopped, then Rynch's head came up as he heard a very faint sound. Not a beast's cry—or was it?

Again those fingers moved on the panel. Was the other sending a message by that means? Rynch watched him check the webbing, count the equipment at his belt, settle the needler in the crook of his arm. Then the stranger left the stream, headed towards the woods.

Rynch jumped to his feet, a cry of warning shaping, but not to be uttered. He padded after the other. There was plenty of time to stop the man before he reached the danger which might lurk under the trees.

However the other was as wary of that dark as if he suspected what might lie in wait there. He angled along northward, avoiding clumps of scattered brush, keeping in the open where Rynch dared not tail him too closely.

Their course, parallel to the woods, brought them at last to a second stream, the size of a river, into which the first creek emptied. Here the other settled down between two rocks with every indication of remaining there for a period.

Thankfully Rynch found his own lurking place from which he could keep the other in sight. The light points gathered, hung in a small luminous cloud over the rocks. But Rynch had prudently withdrawn under a bush, and the scent of its aromatic leaves must have discouraged the sparks, for no such crown came to his sentry post.

Drugged with fatigue, the younger man slept, awaking to full day, a fog of bewilderment and disorientation. To open his eyes to this blue-green pocket instead of to four dirty walls, was wrong.

Remembering, he started up and slunk down the slope, angry at his failure. He found the other's track, not turning back as he had half feared, cleanly printed on level spots of wet earth—eastward now. What was the purpose of the other's expedition? Was he going to use the open cut through which the river ran as a way of penetrating the wooded country?

Now Rynch considered the problem from his own angle. The man from the spacer had made no effort to conceal his trail, in fact it would almost seem that he had deliberately gone out of his way to leave boot prints on favorable stretches of ground. Did he guess that Rynch lurked behind, was now leading him on for some purpose of his own? Or were those traces left to guide another party from the camp?

To advance openly up the stream bed was to invite discovery. Rynch surveyed the nearer bank. Clumps of small trees and high growing bushes dotted that expanse, an ideal cover.

He was hardly out of sight of the bush which had sheltered him when he heard the coughing roar of a water-cat. And the feline was attacking an enemy, enraged to the pitch of vocal frenzy. Rynch ran a zigzag course from one clump of bush to the next. That sound of snarling, spitting hate ended in mid-cry as Rynch crawled to the river bank.

The man from the spacer camp had been the focus of a three-prong attack from a female and her cubs. Three red bodies were flat and still on the gravel as the off-worlder leaned back against a rock breathing heavily. As Rynch sighted him, he stooped to recover the needler he had dropped, lurched away from the rock towards the water, and so blundered straight into another Jumalan trap.

His unsteady foot advancing for another step came down on a slippery surface, and he fell forward as his legs were engulfed in the trap burrow of a strong-jaws. With a startled cry the man dropped the needler again, clawed at the ground about him. Already he was buried to his knees, then his mid-thighs, in the artificial quicksand. But he had not lost his head and was jerking from side to side in an effort to pull free.

Rynch got to his feet, walked with slow deliberation down to the river's brink. The trapped prisoner had shied halfway around, stretching out his arms to find a firmer grip on some rock large and heavy enough to anchor him. After his first startled cry he had made no sound, but now, as he sighted Rynch, his eyes widened and his lips parted.

The box on his chest caught on a stone he had dragged to him in a desperate try for support. There was a spitting of sparks and the stranger worked frantically at the buckle of the webbing harness to loosen it and toss the whole thing from him. The box struck one of the dead water-cats, flashed as fur and flesh were singed.

Rynch watched dispassionately before he caught the needler, jerking it away from the prisoner. The man eyed him steadily, and his expression did not alter even when Rynch swung the off-world weapon to center its sights on the late owner.

"Suppose," Rynch's voice was rusty sounding in his own ears, "we talk now."

The man nodded. "As you wish, Brodie."

CHAPTER SIX

"Brodie?" Rynch squatted on his heels.

Those gray eyes, so light in the other's deeply tanned face, narrowed the smallest fraction, Rynch noted with an inner surge of triumph.

"Were you looking for me?" he added.

"Yes."

"Why?"

"We found an L-B—we wondered if there were survivors."

Slowly Rynch shook his head. "No—you knew I was here. Because you brought me!" He fashioned his suspicions into one quick thrust.

This time there was not the slightest hint of self-betrayal from the other.

"You see," Rynch leaned forward, but still well out of reach from the captive, "I remember!"

Now there was a faint flicker of answer in the man's eyes. He asked quietly:

"What do you remember, Brodie?"

"Enough to know that I am not Brodie. That I did not get here on the L-B, did not build that camp."

He ran one hand over the stock of the needler. Whatever motive lay behind this weird game into which he had been unwillingly introduced, he was now sure that it was serious enough to be dangerous.

"You have no cup this time."

"So you do remember." The other accepted that calmly. "All right. That need not necessarily spoil our plans. You have nothing to return to on Nahuatl—unless you *liked* the Starfall." His voice was icy with contempt. "To play our roles will be for your advantage, too." He paused, his gaze centering on Rynch with the intensity of one willing the desired answer out of his inferior.

Nahuatl. Rynch caught at that. He had been on or in Nahuatl—a planet? a city? If he could make this man believe he remembered everything clearly, more than just the scattered patches that he did....

"You had me planted here, then came back to hunt me. Why? What makes Rynch Brodie so important?"

"Close to a billion credits!" The man from the spacer leaned well back in the hole, his arms spread flat out on either side to keep his body from sinking deeper. "A billion credits," he repeated softly.

Rynch laughed. "You'll have to think of a better one than that, fly-boy."

"The stakes would have to be high, wouldn't they, for us to go to all this staging? You've been conditioned, Brodie, illegally brain-channeled!"

To Rynch the words meant nothing. If they ever had, that was gone, lost in the maze of other things which had been blotted out of his mind by the Brodie past. But he would not give the other the advantage of knowing his uncertainty.

"You need a Brodie for a billion credits. But you don't have a Brodie now!"

To his surprise the prisoner in the earth trap laughed. "I'll have a Brodie when he's needed. Think about a good share of a billion credits, boy, keep thinking of that hard."

"I will."

"Thoughts alone won't work it, you know." For the first time there was a hint of some emotion in the man's voice.

"You mean I need you? I don't think so. I've stopped being a plaque for someone to play across the board." That expression brought another momentary flash of hazy memory—a smoky, crowded room where men slid counters back and forth across tables—not one of Brodie's edited recalls, but his own.

Rynch stood up, started for the rise of the slope, but before he topped that he glanced back. The damaged com box still smoked where its wearer had flung it. Now the man was already straining forward with both arms, trying to reach a rock just a finger space beyond. Lucky for him the burrow was an old one, uninhabited. In time he should be able to work his way out. Meanwhile there was the whole of a wide countryside in which Rynch could discover a hideout—no one would find him now against his will.

He tried, as he strode along, to piece together more of his memories and the scanty information he had had from the Nahuatl man. So he had been "brain-channeled," given a set of false memories to fit a Rynch Brodie whose presence on this world meant a billion credits for someone. He could not believe that this was the spaceman's game alone, for hadn't he spoken of "we"?

A billion credits! The sum was fantastic, the whole story unbelievable.

There was a hot stab of pain on his instep. Rynch cried out, stamped hard. One of the clawed scavengers was crushed. The man leaped back in time to avoid another step into a swarming mass of them at work on some unidentifiable carrion. Staring down at the welter of scaled, segmented bodies and busy claws, he gasped.

Three dead water-cats were near the man trapped in the pit. Bait to draw these voracious eaters straight to the prisoner. Rynch's empty stomach heaved. He swung around, ran across the grassy verge of the upper bank, hoping he was not too late.

As he half fell, half slid down to the water, he saw that the man had managed to hook the webbing of the smouldering box to him, was casting it out and dragging it back patiently, aiming at the nearest rock of size, fruitlessly attempting to hitch its straps over the round of stone.

Rynch dashed on, caught at that loop of webbing, and dug his heels into the loose gravel as he began a steady pull. With his aid the other crawled out, lay panting. Rynch grabbed the man's shoulder, jerked him away from the body of the female water-cat. He was sure he had seen a telltale scurrying around the smaller of the dead cubs.

The man straightened, glanced toward Rynch who was backing off, the needler up and ready between them.

"My turn to ask why?"

Then his gaze followed Rynch's. The smallest cub twitched from side to side. Not with any faint trace of life, but under the attack of the scavengers. More scuttled towards the second cub.

"Thanks!" The stranger was on his feet. "My name is Ras Hume. I don't think I told you that when we last met."

"This doesn't make any difference. I'm not your man, not Brodie!"

Hume shrugged. "You think about it, Brodie, think about it with care. Come back to camp with me and—"

"No!" Rynch interrupted. "You go your way, I go mine from here on."

Again the other laughed. "Not so simple as all that, boy. We've started something which can't just be turned off as easily as you snap down a switch." He took a step or two in Rynch's direction.

The younger man brought up the needler. "Stay right where you are! Your game, Hume? All right, you play it— but not with me."

"And what are you going to do, take to the woods?"

"What I do is my business, Hume."

"No, my business, too, very much so. I'm giving you a warning, boy, in return for your help here." He nodded at the pit. "There's something in that woods—something which didn't show up when the Guild had their survey exploration here."

"The watchers." Rynch retreated step by step, keeping the needler ready. "I saw them."

"You've seen them!" Hume was eager. "What do they look like?"

In spite of his desire to be rid of Hume, Rynch found himself answering that in detail, discovering that on demand he could recall minutely the description of the animal hiding in the tree, the one who had waited in the shelter, and those he had glimpsed drawing in about the L-B clearing.

"No intelligence." Hume turned his head to survey the distant wood. "The verifier reported no intelligence."

"These watchers—you don't know them?"

"No. Nor do I like what you've seen of them, Brodie. So I'm willing to call a truce. The Guild believed Jumala an open planet, our records accredited it so. If that is not true we may be in for bad trouble. As an Out-Hunter I am responsible for the safety of three civs back there in the safari camp."

Hume made sense, much as Rynch disliked admitting it. And the Hunter must have read something of his agreement in his face for now he nodded and added briskly:

"Best place now is the safari camp. We'll head back at once."

Only time had run out. A noise sounded with a metallic ring. Rynch whirled, needler cocked. A glittering ball about the size of his fist rolled away from contact with a boulder, came to rest in the deep depression of one of Hume's boot tracks. Then another flash through the air, a clatter as a second ball spun across a patch of gravel.

The balls seemed to appear out of the air. Displaying rainbow glints they rolled in a semicircle about the two men. Rynch stooped, then Hume's fingers latched about his wrist, dragging his hand away from the globe. It was only then that he realized that sharp action had detached his attention from that ball he had wanted to take up.

"Don't touch!" Hume barked. "And don't look at that too closely! Come along!" He pulled Rynch forward through the yet unclosed arc of the globe circle.

Hume detoured around the feasting scavengers and brought Rynch with him at a trot. They could hear behind them the plop and tinkle of more globes. Glancing back Rynch saw one fall close to the bodies of the water-cats.

"Wait a minute!" He pulled back against Hume's hold. Here was a chance to see what effect that crystal had on the clawed carrion eater.

There was a change in the crystal: Yellow now, then red—red as the few scraps of fur remaining on the rapidly disappearing body.

"Look!"

The pulsating carpet which had covered the dead feline ceased to move. But towards that spot rolled two more of the globes, approaching the scavengers. Now the clawed things were stirring, dropping away from their prey. They spread out in a patch, moved purposefully forward. Behind them, as guardians might head a flock, rolled three globes, flushing scarlet, then more.

Hume's hand came up. From the cone tip of the ray tube spat a lance of fire, to strike the middle crystal. The beam was reflected into the block of scavengers. Scaled bodies, twisted, crisped, were ash. But the crystal continued to roll at the same pace.

"Move!" Hume's other hand hit Rynch's shoulder, knocked him forward in an impetuous shove which nearly took him off his feet. Both men began to run.

"What—what are those things?" Rynch appealed between panting breaths.

"I don't know—and I don't like their looks. They're between us and the safari camp if we keep to the river—"

"Between us and the river now." Rynch saw that glittering swoop through the air, marked the landing of a ball near the water's edge.

"Might be trying to box us in. But that's not going to work. See—ahead there where that log's caught between two rocks? Run out on that when we reach there and take to the water. I don't think those things can float and if they sink to the bottom that ought to fix them as far as we are concerned."

Rynch ran, still holding the needler. He balanced along the drift log Hume had pointed out and a jump sent him floundering in the brown stream thigh deep. Hume joined him, his face grim.

"Downstream—"

Rynch looked. One shape—two—three—Clearly detailed where matching vegetation gave them no covering camouflage, the watchers had come out of the woods at last. A line of them were walking quietly and upright towards the humans, their blue-green fuzz covering like a mist under the direct rays of the sun. Quiet as they seemed at present, the things out of the Jumalan forest were a picture of sheer brute strength as they moved.

"Let's get out of here—fast!"

The men kept moving, and always after them padded that silent line of green-blue, pushing them farther and farther away from the safari camp, on towards the rising mountain peaks. Just as the globes had shaken the scavengers loose from their meal and sent them marching on, so were the humans being herded for some unknown purpose.

At least, once the march of the beasts began, they saw and heard no more of the globes. And as they reached a curve in the river, Hume stopped, swung around, stood studying the line of decorously pacing animals.

"We can pick them off with the needler or the ray."

The Hunter shook his head. "You don't kill," he recited the credo of his Guild, "not until you are sure. There is a method behind this, and method means intelligence."

Handling of X-tee creatures and peoples was a part of Guild training. In spite of his devious game here on Jumala, Hume was Guild educated and Rynch was willing to leave such decisions to him.

The other held out the ray tube. "Take this, cover me, but don't use it until I say so. Understand?"

He waited only for Rynch's nod before he started, at a deliberate pace which matched that of the beasts, back through the river shallows to meet them. But that advancing line halted, stood waiting in silence. Hume's hands went up, palm out, he spoke slowly in Basic-X-Tee clicks:

"Friend." This was all Rynch could make out of that sing-song of syllables Rynch knew to be a contact pattern.

The dark eye pits continued to stare. A light breeze ruffled the fuzz covering of wide shoulders, long muscular arms. Not a head moved, not one of those heavy, rounded jaws opened to emit any answering sound. Hume halted. The silence was threatening, a portending atmosphere spread from the alien things as might a tangible wave.

For perhaps two breaths they stood so, man facing alien. Then Hume turned, walked back, his face set. Rynch offered him the ray tube.

"Fight our way out?"

"Too late. Look!"

Moving lines of blue-green coming down to the river. Not five or six now—a dozen—twenty. There was a small trickle of moisture down the side of the Hunter's brown face.

"We're penned—except straight ahead."

"But we're going to fight!" Rynch protested.

"No. Move on!"

CHAPTER SEVEN

It was some time before Hume found what he wanted, an islet in midstream lacking any growth and rising to a rough pinnacle. The sides were seamed with crevices and caves which promised protection for one's back in any desperate struggle. And they had discovered it none too soon, for the late afternoon shadows were lengthening.

There had been no attack, just the trailing to herd the men to the northeast. And Rynch had lost the first tight pinch of panic, though he knew the folly of underestimating the unknown.

They climbed with unspoken consent, going clear to the top, where they huddled together on a four-foot tableland. Hume unhooked his distance lenses, but it was toward the rises of the mountains that he aimed them, not along the back trail.

Rynch wriggled about, studied the river and its banks. The beasts there were quiet, blue-green lumps, standing down on the river bank or squatting in the grass.

"Nothing." Hume lowered the lenses, held them before his broad chest as he still watched the peaks.

"What did you expect?" Rynch snapped. He was hungry, but not hungry enough to abandon the islet.

Hume laughed shortly. "I don't know. Only I'm sure they are heading us in that direction."

"Look here," Rynch rounded on him. "You know this planet, you've been here before."

"I was one of the survey team that approved it for the Guild."

"Then you must have combed it pretty thoroughly. How is it that you didn't know about them?" He gestured to their pursuers.

"That is what I would like to ask a few assorted experts right about now," Hume returned. "The verifiers registered no intelligent native life here."

"No native life." Rynch chewed that over, came up with the obvious explanation. "All right—so then maybe our blue-backed friends are imported. Suppose someone's running a private business of his own here and wants to get rid of visitors?"

Hume looked thoughtful. "No." He did not enlarge upon his negative. Sitting down he pulled a cylinder container from a belt loop and shook out four tablets, handing two to Rynch, mouthing the others.

"Vita-blocks—good for twenty-four hours sustenance."

The iron rations depended upon by all exploring services did not have the satisfying taste of real food. However Rynch swallowed them dutifully before he descended with Hume to river level. The Hunter splashed water from the stream into a depression in the rock and dropped a pinch of clarifying powder into it.

"With the dark," he announced, "we might be able to get through their lines."

"You believe that?"

Hume laughed. "No—but one doesn't overlook the factor of sheer luck. Also, I don't care to finish up at the place they may have chosen for us." He tilted his chin to study the sky. "We'll take watches and rest in turn. No use trying anything until it is dark—unless they start to move in. You take the first one?"

As Rynch nodded, Hume edged back into a crevice as a shelled creature withdrawing to natural protection, going to sleep as easily as if he could control that state by will. Rynch, watching him curiously for a second or two before climbing up to a position from which he judged he could see all sides of their refuge, determined not to be surprised.

The watchers were crouched down, waiting with that patience which had impressed him from his first sight of the camp sentries back in the forest. There was no movement, no sound. They were simply there—on guard. And Rynch did not believe that the darkness of night would bring any relaxation of that vigilance.

He leaned back, feeling the grit of the rocky surface against his bare back and shoulders. Under his hand was the most efficient and formidable weapon known to the frontier worlds, from this post he could keep the enemy under surveillance and think.

Hume had had him planted here, in the first place, provided with the memory of Rynch Brodie—the reward for him was to be a billion credits. Too much staff work had gone into his conditioning for just a small stake.

So Rynch Brodie was on Jumala, and Hume had come with witnesses to find him. Another part of his mind stood aloof now, applauding the clearness of his reasoning. Rynch Brodie was to be discovered a castaway on Jumala. Only, matters had not worked out according to Hume's plan. In the first place he was certain he had not been intended to know that he was not Rynch Brodie. For a fleeting second he wondered why that conditioning had not completely worked, then went back to the problem of his relationship with Hume.

No, the Out-Hunter had expected a castaway who would be just what he ordered. Then this affair of the watchers—creatures the Guild men had not found here a few months ago—Rynch felt a small cold chill along his spine. Hume's game was one thing, something he could understand, but the silent beasts were another and somehow far more disturbing threat.

Rynch edged forward, watching the mist on the water, his brain striving to solve this other puzzle as neatly as he thought he had discovered the reason for his scrambled memories and his being on Jumala.

The mist was an added danger. Thick enough and those watchers could move in under its curtain. A needler was efficient, yes, but it could wipe out only an enemy at which it was aimed. Blind cross sweeping with its darts would only exhaust the clip without results, save by lucky chance.

On the other hand, suppose they could turn that same gray haze to their own advantage—use it to blanket their withdrawal? He was about to go to Hume with that suggestion when he sighted the new move in their odd battle with the aliens.

A wink of light—two more—blinking, following the erratic course by the pull of the stream. All bobbing along toward the rugged coastline of the islet. Those had appeared out of nothingness as suddenly as the globes when this chase had begun.

The globes and the winking lights on the water connected in his mind, argued new danger. Rynch took careful aim, fired a dart at one which had grounded on the pointed tip of the rocks where the river current came together after its division about the island. For the first time Rynch realized those things below were moving *against* the current—they had come upstream as if propelled.

He had fired and the light was still there, two more coming in behind it, so that now there was an irregular cluster of them. And there was activity on the water-washed rocks before them. Just as the scavengers had moved ahead of the globes on land, so now aquatic creatures had come out of the river, were flopping higher on the islet. And those lights were changing color—from white to reddish-yellow.

Rynch scrabbled with one hand in a rock crevice, found a stone he had noted earlier. He hurled that at the cluster of lights. There was a puff of brilliant red, one was gone. Something flopping on the rocks gave a mewling cry and somersaulted back into the water. Then a finger of mist drew between Rynch and the lights which were now only faint, glowing patches. He swung down from his perch, shook Hume awake.

The Out-Hunter made that instant return to full consciousness which was another defense for the men who live long on the rim of wild worlds.

"What—?"

Rynch pulled him forward. The mist had thickened, but there were more of those ominous lights at water level, spreading down both sides of the point, forming a wall. Dark forms moved out of the water ahead of them, flopping on the rocks, pressing higher, towards the ledge where the men stood.

"Those globes—I think they're moving in the river now." Rynch found another stone, took careful aim, and smashed a second one. "The needler has no effect on them," he reported. "Stones do—but I don't know why."

They searched about them in the crevices for more ammunition, laying up a line of fist-sized rocks, while the lights gathered in, spreading farther and farther down the shores of the islet. Hume cried out suddenly, and aimed his ray tube below. The lance of its blast cut the dark as might a bolt of lightning.

With a shrill squeal, a blot shadow detached from the slope immediately below them. A vile, musky scent, now mingled with the stench of burning flesh, set them coughing.

"Water spider!" Hume identified. "If they are driving those out and up at...."

He fumbled at his equipment belt and then tossed an object downward to disintegrate in a shower of fiery sparks. Wherever those sparks touched rock or ground they flared up in tall thin columns of fire, lighting up the nightmare on the rocks and up the ledges.

Rynch fired the needler, Hume's ray tube flashed and flashed again. Things squealed, or grunted, or died silently, while clawing to reach the upper ledges. He could not be sure of the nature of some of those things. One, armed and clawed as the scavengers, was nearly as large as a water-cat. And a furry, man-legged creature, with a double-jawed head, bore also a ring of phosphorescent eyes set in a complete circle about its skull. They were alien life routed out of the water.

"The lights—smash the lights!" Hume ordered.

Rynch understood. The lights had driven these attackers out of the river. Put out the lights and the boiling broth of water dwellers might conceivably return to their homes. He dropped the needler, took up stones and set about the business of finishing off as many of the lights as he could.

Hume fired into the crawling mass, pausing only once to send another of those flame bombs crashing to illuminate the scene. The water creatures bewildered, clumsy out of their element, were so far at his mercy. But their numbers, in spite of the piling dead, were still a dangerous threat.

Rynch tore gapping holes in that line of lights. But he could see, through the mist, more floating sparks, gathering to take their places, perhaps herding before them more water things to attack. Except for those few gaps he had wrought, the islet was now completely enveloped.

"Ahhhh—" Hume's voice arose in a roar of anger and defiance. He stabbed his ray down at a spot just below their ledge. A huge segmented, taloned leg kicked, caught on the edge of the stone at the level of their feet, twisted aloft again and was gone.

"Up!" Hume ordered. "To the top!"

Rynch caught up two handsful of stones, holding them to his chest with his left arm as he made a last cast to see one light puff out in answer. Then they both scrambled on to that small platform at the top of the islet. By the aid of the burning flame-torches the Hunter had set, they could see that most of the rocky slopes below them now squirmed with a horrible mass of water life.

Where Hume had fired his ray there was fierce activity, as the living feasted on the slain and quarreled over the bounty. But from other quarters the crawling advance pressed on.

"I have only one more flame flare," Hume stated.

One more flare—then they would be in the dark with the mist hiding the forward-moving enemy.

"I wonder if they are watching out there?" Rynch scowled into the dark.

"They—or what sent them. They know what they are doing."

"You mean they must have done this before?"

"I think so. That L-B back there—it made a good landing, and there are supplies missing from its lockers."

"Which you removed—" Rynch countered.

"No. There might have been real castaways landed here. Not that we found any trace of them. Now I can guess why—"

"But you Guild men were here, and you didn't run into this!"

"I know." Hume sounded baffled. "Not a sign then."

Rynch threw the last of his stones, heard it clink harmlessly against a rock. Hume balanced an object on the palm of his hand.

"Last flare!"

"What's that? Over there?"

Rynch had sighted the flashing out of the dark from the river bank, making a pattern of flickers which bore no relation to the infernal lights at the water's edge.

Hume's ray tube pointed skyward as he answered with a series of short bursts.

"Take cover!" The call came weirdly out over the water, the tone dehumanized. Hume cupped his mouth with one hand, shouted back:

"We're on top—no cover."

"Then flatten down—we're blasting!"

They flattened, lay almost in each other's arms, curled on that narrow space. Even through his closed eyelids Rynch caught the flash of vivid, man-made lightning crashing first on one side of the islet and then on the other, and sweeping every crawling horror out of life, into odorous ash. The backlash of that blast must have caught the majority of the lights also. For when Rynch and Hume cautiously sat up, they saw only a handful of widely scattered and dulling globes below.

They choked, coughed, rubbed watering eyes as the fumes from the scorched rocks wreathed up about their perch.

"Flitter with life line—above you!"

That voice had come out of what should have been empty air over their heads. A gangling line trailed across their bodies, a line with a safety belt locked to it, and a second was uncoiling in a slow loop as they watched.

In unison they grabbed for those means of escape, buckled the belts about them."Haul away!" Hume called. The lines tightened, their bodies swung up clear of the blasted river island, as their unseen transport headed for the eastern shore.

CHAPTER EIGHT

A subdued but steady light all around him issued from stark gray walls. He lay on his back in an empty cell-room. And he'd better be on the move before Darfu comes to enforce a rising order with a powerful kick or one of these backhanded blows which the Salarkian used to reduce most humans to helpless obedience.

Vye blinked again. But this wasn't his cubby hole at the Starfall, his nose as well as his eyes told him that. There was no hint of uncleanliness or corruption here. He sat up stiffly, looked down at his own body in dull wonder. The only covering on his bare, brown self was a wide, scaled belt and a loin cloth. Clumsy sandals shod his feet, and his legs, up to thigh level, were striped with healing scratches and blotched with bruises.

Painfully, with mental processes as stiff as his arms and his legs, he tried to think back. Sluggishly, memory associated one picture with another.

Last night—or yesterday—Rynch Brodie had been locked in here. And "here" was one of the storage compartments of a spacer belonging to a man named Wass. It had been Wass' pilot in the flitter which snaked them from the river islet where the monsters had besieged them.

This was a concealed, fortified camp—Wass' hideout. And he was a prisoner with a very uncertain future, depending upon the will of the Veep and a man named Hume.

Hume, the Out-Hunter, had shown no surprise when Wass stood up in the lamplight to greet the rescued. "I see you have been hunting." His eyes had moved from Hume to Rynch and back again.

"Yes—but that does not matter!" the Hunter had returned impatiently.

"No? Then what does?"

"This is not a free world, I have to report that. Get my civs off planet before something happens to them!"

"I thought all safari worlds were certified as free," Wass countered.

"This one isn't. I don't know how or why. But that fact has to be reported and the civs lifted—"

"Not so fast." Wass' voice had been quiet, almost gentle. "Such a report would interest the Patrol, would it not?"

"Of course—" Hume began and then stopped abruptly.

Wass smiled. "You see—complications already. I do not wish to explain anything to the Patrol. Nor do you either, my young friend, not when you stop to think about what might result from such explanations."

"There wouldn't have been any trouble if you'd kept away from Jumala." Hume's control had returned; both voice and manner were under tight rein. "Weren't Rovald's reports explicit enough to satisfy you?"

"I have risked a great deal on this project," Wass replied. "Also, it is well from time to time for a Veep to check upon his field operatives. Men do not grow careless when personal supervision is ever in mind. And it is well that I did arrive here, is it not, Hunter? Or would you have preferred remaining on that island? Whether any of our project may be salvaged is a point we must consider. But for the moment we make no moves. No, Hume, your civs will have to take their chances for a time."

"And if there is trouble?" Hume challenged him. "A report of an alien attack will bring in the Patrol quickly enough."

"You forget Rovald," Wass corrected. "The chance that one of your civs can activate and transmit from the spacer is remote, and Rovald will see that it is impossible. You have picked up Brodie, I see."

"Yes."

"No!" What had possessed him at that moment to contradict? He had realized the folly of his outburst the moment Wass had looked at him.

"This becomes more interesting," the Veep had remarked with that deceptive gentleness. "You are Rynch Brodie, castaway from the Largo Drift, are you not? I trust that Out-Hunter Hume has made plain to you our concern with your welfare, Gentlehomo Brodie."

"I'm not Brodie." Having taken the leap into the dangerous truth he was stubborn enough to continue swimming.

"I find this enlightening indeed. If you are not Brodie—then who are you?"

That had been it. At that moment he couldn't have told Wass who he was, explain that his patchwork of memories had gaping holes.

"And you, Out-Hunter," Wass' reptilian regard had moved again to Hume, "perhaps you have an adequate explanation for this discovery."

"None of his doing," he burst out, "I remembered—"

Some inexplicable emotion made Rynch defend Hume then.

Hume laughed, and there was a reckless edge to that sound. "Yes, Wass, your techs are not as good as they pretend to be. He didn't follow the pattern of action they set for him."

"A pity. But there are always errors when one deals with the human factor. Peake!" One of the other three men moved towards them. "You will escort this young man to the spacer, see him safely stowed for the present. Yes, a pity. Now we must see just how much can be salvaged."

Then Vye had been brought into the shop, supplied with a ration container, and left to himself within this bare-walled cabin to meditate upon the folly of talking too freely. Why had he been so utterly stupid? Veeps of Wass' calibre did not swim through the murky channels of the Starfall, but their general breed had smaller but just as vicious representatives there, and he knew the man for what he was, ruthless, powerful and thorough.

A sound, slight, but easily heard in the silent vacuum of the storage cabin, alerted him. The crack of the sliding panel door opened and Vye crouched, his hand cupping the only possible weapon, the ration container. Hume edged through, shut the door behind him. He stood there, his head turned so his ear rested against the wall; obviously he was listening.

"You brain-smoothed idiot!" The Hunter's voice was a thread of whisper. "Why couldn't you have kept that swinging jaw of yours closed last night? Now listen and listen good. This is a slim try, but it's one we have to take."

"We?" Vye was startled into asking.

"Yes, we! By rights I ought to leave you right here to do the rest of your big, brave speechmaking for Wass' benefit. If I didn't need you, that's just what I would do! If it weren't for those civs—" His head snapped back, cheek to panel, he was listening again. After a long moment his whisper came once more. "I don't have time to repeat this. In about five minutes Peake'll be here with rations. I'll leave this door unlatched. There's another storage cabin across the corridor—see if you can hide there, then trick him into getting in here and lock him in. Got it?"

Vye nodded.

"Then—make for the exit port. Here." He snapped a packet loose from his belt. "This is a flare pak, you saw how they worked on the island. When you get on the ramp beyond the atom lamp, throw this. It should hit the camp force barrier. And the result ought to hold their attention. Then you head for the flitter. Understand?"

"Yes."

The flitter, yes, that was the perfect escape. With a camp force barrier on, any fugitive could only break out by going straight up.

Hume gazed at him soberly, listened once more, and then went. Vye counted a slow five before he followed. The cabin across the corridor was open, just as Hume had promised. He slipped inside, waited.

Peake was coming now, the metallic plates on his spaceboots clicking in regular pattern of sound. He earned another ration container and crooked it in his arm as he snapped up the lock bar on the other cabin.

There was an exclamation of surprise. Vye went into action. His hand, backed by all the strength of his thrusting arm, thumped between Peake's shoulders, sending him staggering into the prison compartment. Before the other could recover either his balance or his wits, Vye had the panel shut, the bar locked into place.

He ran down the corridor to the well ladder, swung down its rungs with an agility born of necessity. Then he was in the air lock, getting his bearings. The flitter stood to his left, the flashing atom lamp, where the men were gathered, to his right.

Vye stepped out on the ramp. He wiped his sweating hand across his thigh. There had to be no failures in the tossing of the flare pak.

Choosing a spot, not directly in line with the lamp but near enough to dazzle the men, he hurled it with all the force he could muster. Then he was running down the ramp, forward to the area of the ship.

There was a flash—shouting—Vye curbed the impulse to look back, darted for the flitter. He jerked open the cabin compartment, scrambled into the cramped space behind the pilot's seat, leaving that free for Hume's quick entrance. More shouting—now he saw the lines of fire wavering from earth to sky along the barrier.

A black shape put on a burst of speed, was silhouetted against that flaming wall, then passed the spacer, grabbed at the open cockpit, and slid in behind the controls. Hume pulled the levers with flying fingers. They arose vertically at a pace which practically slapped Vye's stomach up into the lower regions of his throat.

The searing line of at least one blaster reached after them—too slowly, too low. He heard Hume grunt, and they again leaped higher. Then the Hunter spoke:

"Half an hour at the most—"

"The safari camp?

"Yes."

They no longer climbed. The flitter was boring forwards on a projectile flight, into the dark of the night.

"What're those?" Vye suddenly leaned forward.

Had some of the stars across the space void broken free from their fixed orbits? Flecks of light, moving in an arc, headed towards the speeding flitter.

Hume hit a button. Again they arose in a violent leap above those wandering lights. But ahead on this new level more such dots flocked, moving fast to close in on the flyer.

"A straight ram course," Hume muttered, more to himself than Vye.

Again the flyer drove forward in a rising thrust of speed. Then the smooth purr of the propulsion unit faltered, broke into protesting coughs. Hume worked over the controls, beads of sweat showing on his forehead and cheek in the gleam of the cabin light.

"Deading—deading out!"

He brought the flitter around in a wide circle, the purr smoothed out once more in a steady reassuring beat.

"Out run them!"

But Vye feared they were back again on the losing side of a struggle with the unknown alien power. As they had been herded along the river, so now they were being pushed across the sky, towards the mountains. The enemy had followed them aloft!

Some core of stubborn will in Hume would not yet allow him to admit that. Time and time again he climbed higher—always to meet climbing, twisting, spurting lines of lights which reacted on the engine of the flitter and threatened it with complete failure.

Where they were now in relation to Wass' camp or that of the safari, Vye had no idea, and he guessed that Hume could not be too certain.

Hume switched on the flitter's com unit, tried a channel search until he picked up a click of signal—the automatic reply of the safari camp. His fingertip beat out in return the danger warning, then the series of code sounds to give an edited version of what must be guarded against.

"Wass has a man in your camp. His skin is in just as much danger as the rest. He may not relay it to the Patrol, but he'll keep the force barrier up and the civs inside—anything else would be malicious neglect and a murder charge when the Guild check tape goes in. This call is on the spacer tape now and will be a part of that—he can't possibly alter such a report and he knows it. This is the best we can do now—"

"We're close to the mountains, aren't we?"

"Do you know much about this part of the country?" Vye persisted. Hume's knowledge might be their only hope.

"Flew over the range twice. Nothing to see."

"But there has to be something there."

"If there is, it didn't show up during our survey." Hume's voice was dull with fatigue.

"You're a Guild man, you've dealt with alien life forms before—"

"The Guild doesn't deal with intelligent aliens. That's X-Tee Patrol business. We don't land on any planet with unknown intelligent life forms. Why should we court trouble—couldn't run a safari in under those conditions. X-Tee certified Jumala as a wild world, our survey confirmed that."

"Someone or something landed here after you left?"

"I don't believe so. This is too well organized an action. And since we have a satellite guard in space, any ship landing would be taped and recorded. No such record appeared on the Guild screens. One small spacer—such as Wass'—could slip through by knowing procedure—just as he did. But to land all those beasts and equipment they'd need a regular transport. No—this must be native." Hume leaned forward again, flipped a switch.

A small red light answered on the central board.

"Radar warn-off," he explained.

So they wouldn't end up smeared against some cliff face anyway. Which was only small comfort amid terrifying possibilities.

Hume had taken the precaution just in time. The light blinked faster, and the speed of the flyer was checked as the automatic control triggered by the warn-off came into command. Hume's hands were still on the board, but a system of relays put safety devices into action with a speed past that which a human pilot could initiate.

They were descending and had to accept that, since the warn-off, operating for the sake of the passengers, had ruled that move best. The directive would glide the flitter to the best available landing. It was only moments before the shock gear did touch surface. Then the engine was silent.

"This is it," Hume observed.

"What do we do now?" Vye wanted to know.

"Wait—"

"Wait! For what?"

Hume consulted his planet-time watch in the light of the cabin.

"We have about an hour until dawn—if dawn arrives here at the same time it does in the plains. I don't propose to go out blindly in the dark."

Which made sense. Except that to sit here, quietly, in their cramped quarters, not knowing what might be waiting outside, was an ordeal Vye found increasingly harder to bear. Maybe Hume guessed his discomfort, maybe he was following routine procedure. But he turned, thumbed open one of the side panels in Vye's compartment, and dug out the emergency supplies.

CHAPTER NINE

They sorted the crash rations into small packs. A blanket of the water-resistant, feather-heavy Ozakian spider silk was cut into a protective covering for Vye. That piece of tailoring occupied them until the graying sky permitted them a full picture of the pocket in which the flitter had landed. The dark foliage of the mountain growth was broken here by a ledge of dark-blue stone on which the flyer rested.

To the right was a sheer drop, and a land slip had cut away the ledge itself a few feet behind the flitter. There was only a steadily narrowing path ahead, slanting upward.

"Can we take off again?" Vye hoped to be reassured that such a feat was possible.

"Look up!"

Vye backed against the cliff wall, stared up at the sky. Well above them those globes still swam in unwearied circles, commanding the air lanes.

Hume had cautiously approached the outer rim of the ledge, was using his distance glasses to scan what might lie below.

"No sign yet."

Vye knew what he meant. The globes were overhead, but the blue beasts, or any other fauna those balls might summon, had not yet appeared.

Shouldering their packs they started along the ledge. Hume had his ray tube, but Vye was weaponless, unless somewhere along their route he could pick up some defensive and offensive arm. Stones had burst the lights of the islet, they might prove as effective against the blue beasts. He kept watch for any of the proper size and weight.

The ledge narrowed, one shoulder scraped the cliff now as they rounded a pinnacle to lose sight of the flitter. But the globes continued to hover over them.

"We are still traveling in the direction they want," Vye speculated.

Hume had gone to hands and knees to negotiate an ascent so steep he had to search for head and toe holds. When they were safely past that point they took a breather, and Vye glanced aloft again. Now the sky was empty.

"We may have arrived, or are about to do so," said Hume.

"Where?"

Hume shrugged. "Your guess is as good as mine. And both of us can be wrong."

The steep ascent did not quite reach the top of the cliff around the face of which the ledge curled. Instead their path now leveled off and began to widen out so that they could walk with more confidence. Then it threaded into a crevice between two towering rock walls and sloped downward.

A path unnaturally smooth, Vye thought, as if shaped to funnel wayfarers on. And they came out on the rim of a valley, a valley centered with a wood-encircled lake. They stepped from the rock of the passage onto a springy turf which gave elastically to their tread.

Vye's sandal struck a round stone. It started from its bed in the black-green vegetation, turned over so that round pits stared eyelessly up at him. He was faced by the fleshless grin of a human skull.

Hume went down on one knee, examined the ground growth, gingerly lifted the lace of vertebrae forming a spine. That ended in a crushed break which he studied briefly before he laid the bones gently back into the concealing cover of the mossy stuff.

"That was done by teeth!"

The cup of green valley had not changed, it was the same as it had been when they had emerged from the crevice. But now every clump of trees, every wind-rippled mound of brush promised cover.

Vye moistened his lips, diverted his eyes from the skull.

"Weathered," Hume said slowly, "must have been here for seasons, maybe planet years."

"A survivor from the L-B?" Yet this spot lay days of travel from that clearing back in the plains.

"How did he get here?"

"Probably the same way we would have, had we not holed up on that river island."

Driven! Perhaps the lone human on Jumala herded up into this dead-end valley by the globes or the blue beasts. "This process must have been in action for some time."

"Why?"

"I can give you two reasons." Hume studied the nearest trees narrowly. "First—for some purpose, whatever we are up against wants all interlopers moved out of the lowlands into this section, either to imprison them, or to keep them under surveillance. Second—" He hesitated.

Vye's own imagination supplied a second reason, a revolting one he tried to deny to himself even as he put it into words:

"That broken spine—food...." Vye wanted Hume to contradict him, but the Hunter only glanced around, his expression already sufficient answer.

"Let's get out of here!" Vye was fighting down panic with every ounce of control he could summon, trying not to bolt for the crevice. But he knew he could not force himself any farther into that sinister valley.

"If we can!" Hume's words lingered direly in his ears.

Stones had smashed the globes by the river. If they still waited out there Vye was willing to try and break them with his bare hands, should escape demand such action. Hume must have agreed with those thoughts, he was already taking long strides back to the cliff entrance.

But that door was closed. Hume's foot, raised for the last step toward the crevice corridor, struck an invisible obstruction. He reeled back, clutching at Vye's shoulder.

"Something's there!"

The younger man put out his hand questingly. What his fingers flattened against was not a tight, solid surface, but rather an unseen elastic curtain which gave a little under his prodding and then drew taut again.

Together they explored by touch what they could not see. The crevice through which they had entered was now closed with a curtain they could not pierce or break. Hume tried his ray tube. They watched thin flame run up and down that invisible barrier, but not destroy it.

Hume relooped the tube. "Their trap is sprung."

"There may be another way out!" But Vye was already despondently sure there was not. Those who had rigged this trap would leave no bolt holes. But because they were human and refused to accept the inevitable without a fight, the captives set off, not down into the curve of the cup, but along its slope.

Tongues of brush and tree clumps brought about detours which forced them slowly downward. They were well away from the crevice when Hume halted, flung up a hand in silent warning. Vye listened, trying to pick up the sound which had alarmed his companion.

It was as Vye strained to catch a betraying noise that he was first conscious of what he did not hear. In the plains there had been squeaking, humming, chitterings, the vocalizing of myriad grass dwellers. Here, except for the sighing of the wind and a few insect sounds—nothing. All inhabitants bigger than a Jumalan fly might have long ago been routed out of the land.

"To the left." Hume faced about.

There was a heavy thicket there, too stoutly grown for anything to be within its shadow. Whatever moved must be behind it.

Vye looked about him frantically for anything he could use as a weapon. Then he grabbed at the long bush knife in Hume's belt sheath. Eighteen inches of tri-fold steel gleamed wickedly, its hilt fitting neatly into his fist as he held it point up, ready.

Hume advanced on the bush in small steps, and Vye circled to his left a few paces behind. The Hunter was an expert with ray tube; that, too, was part of the necessary skill of a safari leader. But Vye could offer other help.

He shrugged out of the blanket pack he had been carrying on his back, tossed that burden ahead.

Out of cover charged a streak of red, to land on the bait. Hume blasted, was answered by a water-cat's high-pitched scream. The feline writhed out of its life in a stench of scorched fur and flesh. As Vye retrieved his clawed pack Hume stood over the dead animal.

"Odd." He reached down to grasp a still twitching foreleg, stretched the body out with a sudden jerk.

It was a giant of its species, a male, larger than any he had seen. But a second look showed him those ribs starting through mangy fur in visible hoops, the skin tight over the skull, far too tight. The water-cat had been close to death by starvation; its attack on the men probably had been sparked by sheer desperation. A starving carnivore in a land lacking the normal sounds of small birds and animal life, in a valley used as a trap.

"No way out and no food." Vye fitted one thought to another out loud.

"Yes. Pin the enemy up, let them finish off one another."

"But why?" Vye demanded.

"Least trouble that way."

"There are plenty of water-cats down on the plains. All of them couldn't be herded up here to finish each other off; it would take years—centuries."

"This one's capture may have been only incidental, or done for the purpose of keeping some type of machinery in working order," Hume replied. "I don't believe this was arranged just to dispose of water-cats."

"Suppose this was started a long time ago, and those who did it are gone, so now it goes on working without any real intelligence behind it. That could be the answer, couldn't it?"

"Some process triggers into action when a ship sets down on this portion of Jumala, maybe when one planet's under certain conditions only? Yes, that makes sense. Only why wasn't the first Patrol explorer flaming in here caught? And the survey team—we were here for months, cataloguing, mapping, not a whisper of any such trouble."

"That dead man—he's been here a long time. And when did the Largo Drift disappear?"

"Five—six years ago. But I can't give you any answers. I have none."

It began as a low hum, hardly to be distinguished from the distant howling of the wind. Then it slid up scale until the thin wail became an ululating scream torturing the ears, dragging out of hiding those fears of a man confronting the unknown in the dark.

Hume tugged at Vye, drew the other by force back into the brush. Scratched, laced raw by the whip of branches, they stood in a small hollow with the drift of leaves high about their ankles. And the Hunter pulled into place the portions of growth they had dislodged in their passage into the thicket's heart. Through gaps they could see the opening where lay the body of the water-cat.

The wail was cut off short, that cessation in itself a warning. Vye's body, touching earth with knee and hand as he crouched, picked up a vibration. Whatever came towards them walked heavily.

Did the smell of death draw it now? Or had it trailed them from the closed gate? Hume's breath hissed lightly between his teeth. He was sighting the ray tube through a leaf gap.

A snuffling, heavier than a man's panting. A vast blot, which was neither clearly paw nor hand, swept aside leaves and branches on the other side of the small clearing, tearing them casually from the shrubs.

What shuffled into the open might be a cousin of the blue beasts. But where they had given only an impression of brutal menace, this was savagery incarnate. Taller than Hume, but hunched forward in its neckless outline, the thing was a monster. And over the round of the lower jaw, tusks protruded in ugly promise.

Being carnivorous and hungry, it scooped up the body of the water-cat and fed without any prolonged ceremony.

Vye, remembering the crushed spine of the human skeleton, was sickened.

Done, it reared on hind feet once again, the pear-shaped head swung in their direction. Vye was half certain he had seen that tube-nose expand to test the air and scent them.

Hume pressed the button of the ray tube. That soundless spear of death struck in midsection of that barrel body. The thing howled, threw itself in a mad forward rush at their bush. Hume snapped a second blast at the head, and the fuzz covering it blackened.

Missing them by a precious foot, the creature crashed straight on through the thicket, coming to its knees, writhing in a rising chorus of howls. The men broke out of cover, raced into the open where they took refuge behind a chimney of rock half detached from the parent cliff. Down the slope the bushes were still wildly agitated.

"What was that?" Vye got out between sobbing breaths.

"Maybe a guardian, or a patrol stationed to dispose of any catch. Probably not alone, either." Hume fingered his ray tube. "And I am down to one full charge—just one."

Vye turned the knife he held around in his fingers, tried to imagine how one could face up to one of those tusked monsters with only this for a weapon. But if that thing had companions, none were coming in answer to its dying wails. And after it had been quiet for a while Hume motioned them out of hiding.

"From now on we'll keep to the open, better see trouble like that before it arrives. And I want to find a place to hole up for the night."

They trailed along the steep upper slope and in time found a place where a now dried stream had once formed a falls. The empty watercourse provided an overhang, not quite a cave, but shelter. Gathering brush and stones, they made a barricade and settled behind it to eat sparingly of their rations.

"Water—a whole lake of it down there. The worst of it is that a water supply in a dry country is just where hunters congregate. That lake's entirely walled in by woodland and provides cover for a thousand ambushes."

"We might find a way out before our water bulbs fail," Vye offered.

Hume did not answer directly. "A man can live for quite a while on very thin rations, and we have tablets from the flitter emergency supplies. But he can't live long without water. We have two bulbs. With stretching that is enough for two days—maybe three."

"We ought to get completely around the cliffs in another day."

"And if we do find a way out, which I doubt, we're still going to need water for the trek out. It's right down there waiting until our need is greater than either our fear or our cunning."

Vye moved impatiently, his blanket-clad shoulders scraping the rock at their backs. "You don't think we have a chance!"

"We aren't dead. And as long as a man is breathing, and on his feet, with all his wits in his skull, he always has a chance. I've blasted off-world with odds stacked high on the other side of the board." He flexed that plasta-flesh hand which was so nearly human and yet not by the fraction which had changed the course of his life. "I've lived on the edge of the big blackout for a long time now—after a while you can get used to anything."

"One thing I would like—to get at the one who set this trap," commented Vye.

Hume laughed with dry humor. "After me, boy, after me. But I think we might have to wait a long time for that meeting."

CHAPTER TEN

Vye crawled weakly from the area of a rock outcrop. The sun, reflected from the cliff side, was a lash of fire across his emaciated body. His swollen tongue moved a pebble back and forth in his dry mouth. He stared dimly down the slope to that beckoning platter of water open under the sun, rimmed with the deadly woodland.

What had happened? They had gone to sleep that first night under the ledge of the dried waterfall. And all of the next day was only a haze to him now. They must have moved on, though he could remember nothing, save Hume's odd behavior—dull-eyed silence while stumbling on as a brainless servio-robot, incoherent speech wherein all the words came fast, running together unintelligibly. And for himself—patches of blackout.

At some time they had come to the cave and Hume had collapsed, not rousing in answer to any of Vye's struggles to awaken him. How long they had been there Vye could not tell now. He had the fear of being left alone in this place. With water perhaps Hume could be returned to consciousness, but that was all gone.

Vye believed he could scent the lake, that every breeze up slope brought its compelling enticement. Just in case Hume might awake to a state of semi-consciousness and wander off, Vye tethered him with blanket bonds.

Vye fingered Hume's knife, which had been painstakingly lashed to a trimmed shaft of wood. Since he had emerged from that clouding of mind which still gripped the Hunter, he had done what he could to prepare for another attack from any roving beast. And he also had Hume's ray tube—its single charge to be used only in dire need.

Water! His cracked lips moved, ejected the pebble. Their four empty water bulbs were in the front of his blanket tunic, pressing against his ribs. It was now—or die, because soon he would be too weak to make the attempt at all. He darted for the first stand of bush downhill.

As the brooding silence of the valley continued, he reached the edge of the wood unhindered, intent on his mission with a concentration which shut out everything save his need and the manner of satisfying it.

He squatted in the bush, eyeing the length of woodland ahead. Then he tried the only action he had been able to think out. That beast Hume had killed had been too heavy to swing up in trees. But Vye's own weight now did not prohibit that form of travel.

With spear and ray tube firmly attached to him, Vye climbed into the first tree. A slim chance—but his only defense against a possible ambush. A wild outward swing brought him, heart-thudding, to the next set of limbs. Then he had a piece of luck, a looped vine tied together a whole group of branches from one treetop to the next.

Hand grips, balance, sometimes a walk along a branch—he threaded towards the lake. Then he came to a gap. With hands laced into tendrils, Vye hunched to look down on a beaten ribbon of gray earth—a trail well used by the evidence of its pounded surface.

That area had to be crossed on foot, but his passage through the brush below would leave traces. Only—there was no other way. Vye checked the lashings of his weapons again before leaping. Almost in the same instant his sandals hit the packed earth he was running. His palms skinned raw on rough bark as he somehow scrambled aloft once more.

No more vines, but broad limbs shooting well out. He dropped from one to another-stopped for breath—listened.

The dark gloom of the wood was broken by sunlight. He was at the final ring of trees. To get to the water he must descend again. A dead trunk extended over the water. If he could run out on that and lower the bulb, it could work.

Eerie silence. No flying things, no tree dwelling reptiles or animals, no disturbance of any water creature on the unruffled surface of the lake. Yet the sensation of life, inimical life, lurking in the depths of the wood, under the water, bore in upon him.

Vye made the light leap to the bole of the dead tree, balanced out on it over the water, moving slowly as the trunk settled a little under his weight. He hunkered down, brought out the first bulb tied fast to a blanket string.

The water of the river had been brown, opaque. But here the liquid was not so cloudy. He could see snags of dead branches below its surface.

And something else!

Down in those turgid depths he made out a straight ridge running with a trueness of line which could not be nature's unassisted product. That ridge joined another in a squared corner. He leaned over, strained his eyes to follow through the murk the farther extent of those two ridges. Looked along both pointed protuberances aimed at the surfaces of the lake, like fangs in an open jaw. Down there was something—something artificially fashioned which might be the answer to all their questions. But to venture into the lake himself—he could not do it! If he could bring the Out-Hunter to his senses the other might find the solution to this puzzle.

Vye filled his bulbs, working speedily, but still studying what he could see of the strange erection under the lake. He thought it was curiously free of silt, and its color, as far as he could distinguish, allowing for the dark hue of the water, was light gray—perhaps even white. He lowered his last bulb.

Down in the bleached forest of dead branches, well to one side of the mysterious walls, there was movement, a slow rolling of a shadow so hidden by a stirring of bottom mud that Vye could not make out its true form. But it was rising to the bulb.

Vye hated to lose a single precious drop. Once he might have the luck to make this journey unmolested, a second time the odds could be too high.

A flash—the slowly rising shadow was transformed into a whizzing spear of attack. Vye snapped the bulb out of the water just as a nightmarish, armored head arose on a whiplash of coiled, scaled neck, and a blunt nose thudded against the tree trunk with a hollow boom. Vye clung to his perch as the thing flopped back into deeper water from a froth of beaten foam, leaving a patch of odorous scum and slime to bracelet the waterlogged wood.

He ran for the shelter of the trees to get away. This time there was no rear, no thump of feet in warning. Out of the ground itself, or so it seemed to Vye's startled terror, reared one of the tusked beasts. To reach his tree and its dubious safety he had to wind past that chimera. And the creature waited with a semblance of ease for him to come to it.

Vye brought around his spear. The length of the haft might afford him a fighting chance if he could send the point home in some vulnerable spot. Yet he knew that the beasts were hard to kill.

The mouth opened in a wide grin of menace. Vye noted a telltale tightening of shoulder muscles. It was going to rush for him now with those clawed forepaws out to rip.

To wait was to court disaster. Vye shouted, his battle cry piercing the silence of the lake and wood. He sprang, aiming the spear point at the beast's protuberant belly, and then swerved to the side as the knife bit home, raking his weapon to open a gaping wound.

The spear was jerked from Vye's hold as both those taloned paws closed on it. Then the creature pulled it free, snapped the haft in two. Vye fired a short blast from the ray tube before it could turn on him, saw fur-fuzz afire, as he ran for the tree.

Beneath its branches he looked back. The beast was pawing at the burning fur on its head, and he had perhaps a second or two. He jumped and his fingers caught on the low hanging branch, then he made a superhuman effort, was up out of the path of the thing which rushed blindly for the tree, shrieking in frenzied complaint.

The huge body crashed against the trunk with force which nearly shook Vye from his hold. As the giant forepaws belabored the wood, strove to lift the body from the ground, Vye worked his way out on another branch. In the end it was the shaking of that limb under him which aided his swing to the next tree. And from there he traveled recklessly, intent only on getting out of the woods as fast as he could.

By the noise the beast was still assaulting the tree, and Vye marveled at its vitality, for the belly wound would long ago have killed any creature he knew. Whether it could trace his flight aloft, or whether its howls would bring more of its kind, he could not guess, but every second he could gain was all important now.

At the gap over the trail he hesitated. That path ran in the direction of the open, and to go on foot meant the possibility of greater speed. Vye slipped from the bough, hit the ground, and ran. His ragged lungsful of air came in great gasps and he doubted if he could take the exertion of more tree travel now. He raced down the path.

Those mewling cries were louder, he was sure of it. Now he heard the thump of the beast's blundering pursuit behind him. But its bulk and hurts slowed it. In the open he could find cover behind a rock, use the ray again.

The trees began to thin. Vye summoned power for a last burst of speed, came out of the shadow of the wood as might a dart expelled from a needler. Before him, up slope, was the closed door of the valley. And moving in from the left was another of the blue beasts.

He could not retreat to the trees. But the newcomer was moving with the same ponderous self-confidence its fellow had shown earlier. Vye dodged right, headed for the rocks by the gap. As he pulled himself into that temporary fortification, the wounded beast dragged out of the woods below. He thought it was blind, yet some instinct drove it after him.

Shaking from fatigue, Vye steadied his forearm on the top of the rock, brought up the ray tube. Less than two yards away now was the deceptively open mouth of the gap. If he threw himself at that, would the elasticity of the unseen curtain hurl him back into the claws of the enemy?

He fired his blast at the head of the unwounded beast. It screeched, threw out its arms, and one of those paws struck against its wounded fellow. With a cry, that one flung itself at its companion in the hunt, and they tangled in a body-to-body battle terrible in its utter ferocity. Vye edged along the cliff determined to reach the cave and Hume. And the two blue things seemed intent on finishing each other off.

The one from the wood was done, the fangs of the other ripping out its throat. Tearing viciously the victor made sure of its kill, then its seared head came up, swung about to face Vye. He guessed it was aware of his movements whether it could see or not.

But he was not prepared for the speed of its attacking lunge. Heretofore the creatures had given the impression of brute strength rather than agility. And he had been almost fatally deceived. He jumped backwards, knowing he must elude that attack, for he could not survive hand-to-hand combat with the alien thing.

There was a moment of dazed disorientation, a weird sensation of falling through unstable space in which there had never been and never would be firm footing again. He was rolling across rock—outside the curtain of the gap.

He sat up, the feeling of being adrift in unmeasurable nothingness making him sick, to watch mistily as the blue beast came to a halt. Whimpering it turned, but before it reached the level of the woods, it sagged to its knees, fell face forward and was still, a destructive machine no longer controlled by life.

Vye tried to understand what had happened. He had somehow broken through that barrier which made the valley a prison. For a moment all that mattered was his freedom. Then he looked apprehensively behind him along the road to the open, more than half expecting to see a gathering of the globes, or of the less impressive lowland beasts that acted as herders. But there was nothing.

Freedom! He dragged himself to his feet. Free to go! He slipped Hume's ray tube back into his belt. Hume was still in the valley!

Vye rubbed his shaking hands across his face. Through the barrier and free—but Hume was back there, without a weapon, defenseless against any questing beast able to nose him out. Sickly, without water and protection, he was a dead man even while he still breathed.

Keeping one hand against the wall of the gap in support, Vye started to walk, not out of the gap towards the distant lowlands, but back into the valley, forcing himself to that by his will alone and screaming inside against such suicidal folly. He put out his hand tentatively when he reached the two points of rock where that curtain had hung. There was no obstruction—the barrier was down! He must get back to Hume.

Still keeping his wall hold, Vye lurched through the gate, was once more in the valley. He stood swaying, listening. But once again there was silence, not even the wind moved through trees or bushes. Placing one foot carefully before the other he went on towards Hume's cave. The haze which had clouded his thinking processes since that first morning's awakening in this bowl was gone now. Except for the physical weakness that weighted his body, he felt once more entirely alive and alert.

Wriggling in the cave's entrance was the Hunter. He had freed the bonds Vye had put on his legs, but his hands were still tied. His face, grimy, sweat-covered, was turned up to the sunlight, and his eyes were again bright with reason.

Vye found the strength to run the last few feet between them. He was fumbling with those ties about Hume's

wrists as he blurted out the news. The barrier was out—
they could go.

Then he was bringing one of those precious bulbs,
raising it to Hume's eager mouth, squeezing a portion of its
contents between the man's cracked and bleeding lips.

Somehow they made that trip back to the valley gate.
When they saw their goal, Hume broke from Vye's hold,
tottered forward with a cry not far removed from a sob.
He rebounded to slip full length to the ground and lie
there. Sobbing dryly, his gaunt face, eyes closed, turned up
to the sky. The trap had snapped shut once again.

"Why—why?" Vye found he was repeating the same
words over and over, his gaze blank, unfocussed, yet
turned to the woods of the lake.

"Tell me what happened again."

Vye's head came around. Hume had pulled himself up
so that his shoulders rested against the rock wall. His
plasta-hand was out-flung, slipping up and down what
seemed empty air, but which was the barrier against
freedom. And now his eyes seemed entirely sane.

Slowly, hesitating between words, Vye went over the full
account of his visit to the lake, his retreat before the beasts,
his fortunate stumble through the gap.

"But you came back."

Vye flushed. He was not going to try to explain that.
Instead he said:

"If it went away once, it can again."

Hume did not press the subject of his return. Rather he
fastened upon the end of that action with the wounded
beast, made Vye go through it verbally a third time.

"There is just this," he said when the other was done.
"When you fell you were not thinking of the barrier at

all—and your wits were working again. You had come out of the daze we both had."

Vye tried to remember, decided that the Hunter was correct. He had been trying to elude the charge of the beast, only, fear and that desperate desire had occupied his mind at that moment. But what did that signify?

To test just what he did not know, he crawled now to Hume's side, put up his own hand to the space where the plasta-flesh palm slid back and forth on nothingness. But he almost fell on his face, forward into the gap. Where he had been expecting the resistance of the unseen curtain there had been nothing at all! He turned to Hume with the expression of a man who had been stunned by an unexpected blow.

CHAPTER ELEVEN

It is open for you!" Hume broke the quiet first. His eyes were very bleak in his bony face.

Vye stood up, took one step and was on the other side of the curtain where Hume's hand still found substance. He came back with the same lack of hindrance. Yes, to him there was no longer a barrier. But why—why him when Hume was still a prisoner?

The Hunter raised his head so his eyes could meet Vye's with the authority of an order. "Go, get away while you can!"

Instead Vye dropped down beside the other. "Why?" he asked baldly. And then the most obvious of all answers came.

He glanced at Hume. The Hunter's head lolled back against the rock which supported him, his eyes were closed now, and he had the look of a man who had been driven to the edge of endurance and was now willing to relinquish his grip and let go.

Deliberately Vye brought up his right hand, balled his fingers into a fist. And just as deliberately he struck home, square on the point of that defenseless chin. Hume sagged, would have slipped down the surface of the rock had Vye's hands not caught in his armpits.

Since he had not the strength left to get to his feet with such a burden, Vye crawled, dragging the inert body of the Hunter with him. And this time, as he had hoped, there was no resistance at the gap. Unconscious, Hume was able to cross the barrier. Vye stretched him as comfortably flat as he could, used a portion of their water on his face until he moaned, muttered, and raised his hand feebly to his head.

Then those gray eyes opened, focussed on Vye.

"What—"

"We're both through now, both of us!" The younger man saw Hume glance around him with waking belief.

"But how—?"

"I knocked you out, that's how," Vye returned.

"Knocked me out? I crossed when I was unconscious!" Hume's voice steadied, strengthened. "Let me see!" He rolled over on his side, threw out his arm, and this time the hand found no wall. For him, too, the barrier was gone.

"Once through, you are free," he added wonderingly. "Maybe they never foresaw any escapes." He struggled up, sitting with his hands hanging loosely between his knees.

Vye turned his head, looked down the trail. The length of distance lying between them and the safari camp now faced them with a new problem. Neither of them could make that trek on foot.

"We're out, but we aren't back—yet," Hume echoed his thought.

"I was wondering, if *this* door is open—" Vye began.

"The flitter!" Again Hume's mind matched his. "Yes, if those globes aren't hanging around just waiting for us to try."

"They might act only to get us here, not to keep us once we're in." That might be wishful thinking, they wouldn't know until they tried to prove it.

"Give me a hand." Hume held out his own, let Vye pull him to his feet. Weak as he was, he was clear-eyed, plainly clear-headed once more. "Let's go!"

Together they went back through the gap, then tested the absence of the barrier once more, to make sure. Hume laughed. "At least the front door remains open, even if we find the back one closed."

Vye left him sitting by that entrance while he made a quick trip to the cave to pick up the small pack of supplies left them. When he returned they crammed tablets into their mouths, drank feverishly of the lake water, and, with the stimulation of the new energy, set off along the cliff face.

"This wall in the lake," Hume asked suddenly, "you are sure it is artificial?"

"Runs too straight to be anything else, and those projections are evenly spaced. I don't see how it could be natural."

"We'll have to be sure."

Vye thought of that attacking water creature. "No diving in there," he protested. Hume smiled, a stretch of skin far too tight over his jaw now.

"Not us, at least not us now," he agreed. "But the Guild will send another survey."

"What could be the reason for all this?" Vye helped his companion over the loose debris of a cliff slide.

"Information."

"What?"

"Someone—or something—picked our brains while we were out of our heads. Or—" Hume paused suddenly, looked directly at Vye. "I have a vague feeling that you were able to keep going a lot better than I was. That so?"

"Some of the time," Vye admitted.

"That checks. Part of me knew what was going on, but was helpless while that other thing," his smile of moments earlier was wiped away, there was a chill edge in his voice, "picked over my brains, sorted out what it wanted."

Vye shook his head. "I didn't feel that way. Just thick-headed—as if I were sleep walking and yet awake."

"So it took me over, but didn't go all the way with you. Why? Another question for our list."

"Maybe—maybe Wass' techs fixed it so I couldn't be brain-picked, as you call it," Vye offered.

Hume nodded. "Could be—would well be. Come on." He pressed the pace now.

Vye turned to look down the slope suspiciously. Had Hume another warning of menace out of the wood? He could sight no movement there. And from this distance the lake was a topaz sheet of calm which could hide anything. Hume was already several paces ahead, scrambling as if the valley monsters were again on their track.

"What's the matter?" Vye demanded, as he caught up.

"Night coming." Which was true. Then Hume added, "If we can reach the flitter before sunset, we'll have a chance to fly over the lake down there, to make a taping of it before we go."

The energy of the tablets strengthened them so that by the time they reached the crevice door they were moving with their former agility. For a single second Hume hesitated before that slit, almost as if he feared the test he must make. Then he stepped forward and this time into freedom.

They reached the ledge where the flitter perched just as they had seen it last. How long ago that had been they could not have told, but they suspected that days of haze hung in between. Vye searched the sky. No globes winking there—just the flyer alone.

He took his old seat behind the pilot, watched Hume test the relays and responses in the quick run down of a man who has done this chore many times before. But the other gave a little sigh of relief when he finished.

"She's all right, we can lift."

Again they both looked aloft, half fearing to see those malignant herders wink into being to forbid flight. But the sky was as serenely clear of even a drifting cloud as they could hope. Hume pressed a button and they arose vertically with an even progress totally unlike the leap which had taken them out of Wass' camp.

Well above the cliff wall they hovered, and were able to see below the round bowl of the valley prison. Hume touched controls, the flitter descended slowly just above the center of the lake. And from this position they were able to sight the other peculiarity of that body of water, that it was perfectly oval in shape, far too perfect to be an undeveloped product of nature. Hume took a round disk from his equipment belt, fitted it carefully into a slot on the control board and pressed the button below. Then he sent the flitter in a weaving zigzag course well above the surface of the water, so that eventually the flyer passed over every foot of its surface.

And from above, in spite of the turgid quality of the liquid, they could see what did rest on the bottom of that oval. The wall with its sharp corner which Vye had noted from shore level was only part of a water covered erection. It made a design when seen from overhead, a six-pointed star surrounding an oval and in the midst of that oval a black blot which they could not identify.

Hume brought the flitter over in one last sweep. "That's it. We have a full taping."

"What do you think it is?"

"A device set there by an intelligent being, and set a long time ago. This valley wasn't arranged over night, six months ago—or even a year ago. We'll have to let the experts tell us when and for what reason. Now, let's head for home!"

He brought the flitter up and over the valley wall, flying southwest so that they passed over the gap which was the main entrance to the trap. And now he tried the com unit, endeavoring to pick up a signal on which they could beam in for a safe ride.

"That's odd." Under Hume's control the direction finder passed back and forth without bringing any answering code click from the mike. "We may be too far in the mountains to pick up the beam. I wonder...." He swept the needle in another direction, slightly to the left.

A crackle spat from the mike. Vye could not read code but the very fury and intensity of that sound suggested panic—even terror.

"What's that?"

Hume spoke without looking away from the control board. "Alarm."

"From the safari?"

"No. Wass." For a long second Hume sat very still, his fingers quiet. The flitter was on the automatic course, taking them out of the mountains, and Vye thought that their air speed was such they were already well removed from that sinister valley.

Hume made a slight adjustment to a dial, and the flitter banked, coming around on another course. Once more he spun the finder of the com. This time he was answered with a series of well-spaced clicks which lacked the urgency of that other call. Hume listened until the code rattled into silence again.

"They're all right at the safari camp."

"But Wass is in trouble. So what does that matter?" Vye wanted to know.

"It matters this much." Hume spoke slowly as if he must convince himself as well as Vye. "I'm the Guild man on Jumala, and the Guild man is responsible for all civs."

"You can't call him your client!"

Hume shook his head. "No, he's no client. But he's human."

It narrowed down to that when a man was on the frontier worlds—humans stood together. Vye wanted to deny it, but his own emotions, as well as the centuries of age-old tradition, argued him down. Wass was a Veep, one of the criminal parasites dabbling in human misery along more than one solar lane. But he was also human and, as one of their own species, had his claim on them.

Vye watched Hume take over the controls, felt the flitter answer another change of course, then heard the frantic yammer of the distress call as they leveled off to ride its beam in to the hidden camp.

"Automatic." Hume had turned down the volume of the receiver so that the clicks in the mike no longer were so strident. "Set on maximum and left that way."

"They had a force barrier around the camp and they knew about the globes and the watchers." Vye tried to imagine what had happened in that woods clearing.

"The barrier might have shorted. And without the flitter they would have been pinned."

"Could have taken off in the spacer."

"Wass doesn't have the reputation of letting any project get out of his hands."

Vye remembered. "Oh—your billion credit deal."

To his surprise Hume laughed. "Seems all very far and out of orbit now, doesn't it, Lansor? Yes, our billion credit deal—but that was thought out before we knew there were more players around the table than we counted. I wonder...."

But what he wondered he did not put into words and a moment later he added over his shoulder, "Better try to get some rest, boy. We've some time to a set-down."

Vye did sleep, deeply, dreamlessly. And he roused after a gentle shaking to see a beam of light in the sky ahead, though around them was the solid darkness of night.

"That's a warning," Hume explained. "And I can't raise any reply from the camp except a repeat of the distress call. If there is anyone there now, he can't or won't answer."

Against that column of light they could make out the sky-pointed taper of the spacer and the auto-pilot landed them beside that ship in the middle of an area well lighted by the steady shaft of light from the tripod standing where the atom lamp had been on the night they had made their escape from camp.

Climbing stiffly from the small flyer they advanced with caution. A very few minutes later Hume slid his ray tube back into its belt loop.

"Unless they've holed up in the spacer—and I can't see why they'd do that—this camp's deserted. And they haven't taken any equipment with them except maybe a few items they could back-pack."

The ship proved as empty of life as the campsite. A wall seat pulled out too hastily so that it was jammed awry, the com cabin suggested that the leave-taking, when and for what reason, had been a matter of some emergency. Hume did not touch the tape set to keep on broadcasting the call for assistance.

"What now?" Vye wanted to know as they completed the search.

"The safari camp first—and a call for the Patrol."

"Look here," Vye set down the ration container he had found, was emptying it with vast satisfaction of one who had been too long on tablets, "if you beam the Patrol you'll have to talk, won't you?"

Hume went on fitting new charges into his ray tube. "The Patrol has to have a full report. There's no way of bypassing that. Yes, we'll have to give all the story. You needn't worry." He snapped closed the load chamber. "I can clear you all the way. You're the victim, remember."

"I wasn't thinking about that."

"Boy." Hume tossed the tube up in the air, caught it in his plasta-hand. "I went into this deal with my eyes wide open—why doesn't matter very much now. In fact," he stared beyond Vye out into the empty, lighted camp, "I've begun to wonder about a lot of things—maybe too late. No—we'll call the Patrol and we'll do it not because it is Wass and his men out there, but because we're human and they're human, and there's a nasty set-up here which has already sucked in other humans for its own purposes."

The skeleton in the valley! And how very close they had been themselves to joining that unknown in his permanent residence.

"So now we make time—back to the safari camp. Get our message off to the Patrol and then we'll try to trace Wass and see what we can do. Jumala is off a regular route. The Patrol won't be here tomorrow at sunrise, no matter how much we wish a scouter would planet then."

Vye was quiet as he stowed in the flitter again. As Hume had said, events moved fast. A little while ago he had wanted to settle with this Out-Hunter, wring out of him not only an explanation for his being here, but claim satisfaction for the humiliation of being moved about to suit some others' purposes. Now he was willing to defeat Wass, bring in the Patrol, go up against whatever hid in that lake up there, providing Hume was not the loser. He tried to think why that was so and could not, he only knew it was the truth.

They were both silent as they took off from Wass' deserted camp, sped away over the black blot of the woodland towards the safari headquarters on the plains. There were stars above again but no globes. Just as they had won their freedom from the valley, so they moved without escort on the plains.

But the lights were there—not impinging on the flitter, or patrolling along its line of flight. No, they hung in a glowing cluster ahead when in the dawn the flitter shot away from the woods, headed for the landmark of the safari camp. A crown of lights circled over the camp site, as if those below were in a state of siege.

Hume aimed straight for them and this time the bobbing circle split wide open, broke to left and right. Vye looked below. Though the grayness of the morning was still hardly more than dusk he could not miss those humps spaced at intervals on the land, just beyond the unseen line of the force barrier. The lights above, the beasts below, the safari camp was under guard.

CHAPTER TWELVE

"There is only one way they could be moving—toward the mountains." Hume stood in the open space among the bubble tents, facing him the four men of the camp, the three civs and Rovald. "You say it's been seven days, planet time, since I left here. They may have been five days on that trail. If possible we have to stop them before they reach that valley."

"A fantastic story." Chambriss wore the affronted expression of a man who expected no interference with his own concerns. Then catching Hume's eye he added, "Not that we doubt you, Hunter. We have the evidence in those dumb brutes waiting out there. However, by your own story, this Wass is an outside-the-law Veep, on this planet secretly for criminal purposes. Surely there is no reason for us to risk our safety in his behalf. Are you certain he is in any danger at all? You and this young man here have, by your testimony, been into the enemies' territory and have been able to get out again."

"Through a series of fortunate chances which might never occur again." Hume was patient, too patient, Rovald seemed to think. His hand moved, he was holding a ray tube so that a simple movement of the wrist could send a crisping blast across all the rest of the party.

"I say, stop this yapping and get out there and pick up the Veep!"

"I intend to—after I call the Patrol."

Rovald's tube was now aimed directly at Hume. "No Patrol!" he ordered.

"This wrangling has gone far enough." It was Yactisi who spoke with an authority which startled them all. And as their attention swung to him, he was already in action.

Rovald cried out, the weapon spun from his fingers, fingers which were slowly reddening. Yactisi nodded with satisfaction and he held his electo pole ready for a second attack. Vye scooped up the tube which had whirled across the ground to strike against his borrowed boot.

"I'll set the call for the Patrol, then I'll try to locate Wass," Hume stated.

"Sensible procedure," Yactisi approved in his dry voice. "You believe that you are now immune to whatever force this alien installation controls?"

"It would seem so."

"Then, of course, you must go."

"Why?" Chambriss countered for the second time. "Suppose he isn't so immune after all? Suppose he gets out there and is captured again? He's our pilot—do you want to be planet bound *here*?"

"This man is also a pilot." Starns indicated Rovald, who was nursing his numb hand.

"Since he, too, is one of these criminals, he's not to be trusted!" Chambriss shot back. "Hunter, I demand that you take us off planet at once! And it is only fair to inform you that I also intend to prefer charges against you and against the Guild. Empty world! Just how empty have we found this world?"

"But, Gentlehomo," Starns showed no signs of any emotion but eager curiosity, "to be here at this time is a privilege we could not hope to equal except by good fortune! The T-Casts will be avid for our stories."

What had that to do with the matter, puzzled Vye. But he saw Starns' reminder produce a quick change in Chambriss.

"The T-Casts," he repeated, his expression of anger smoothing away. "Yes, of course, this is, in a manner of speaking, a truly historic occasion. We are in a unique position!"

Had Yactisi smiled? That change of lip line had been so slight Vye could not call it a smile. But Starns appeared to have found the right way to handle Chambriss. And it was the same little man who offered his services in another way when he said, diffidently to Hume:

"I have some experience with coms, Hunter. Do you wish me to send your message and take over the unit until you return? I gather," he added with a certain delicacy, "that it will not be expedient for your gearman to engage in that duty now."

So it was that Starns was installed in the com cabin of the spacer, sending out the request for Patrol aid, while Rovald was locked in the storage compartment of the same ship, pending arrival of those same authorities. As Hume sorted out supplies and Vye loaded them into the waiting flitter, Yactisi approached the Hunter.

"You have a definite plan of search?"

"Just to cast north from their camp. If they've been gone long enough to hit the foothills we may be able to sight them climbing. Otherwise, we'll go all the way up to the valley, wait for them there."

"You don't believe that they will be released after they have been—processed?"

Hume shook his head. "I don't think we would have been free, Gentlehomo, if it hadn't been for a series of fortunate accidents."

"Yes, though you didn't give us many details about that, Hunter."

Hume put down the needler he had been charging. He studied Yactisi across that weapon.

"Who are you?" His voice was soft but carried a snap.

For the first time Vye saw the tall, lean civ really smile.

"A man of many interests, Hunter—shall we let it go at that for the present? Though I assure you that Wass is not one of them in the way you might believe."

Gray eyes met brown, held so straightly. Then Hume spoke. "I believe you. But I have told you the truth."

"I have never doubted that—only the amount of it. There must be more talking later on—you understand that?"

"I never thought otherwise." Hume set the needler inside the flitter. The civ smiled again, this time including Vye in that evidence of good will before he walked away.

Hume made no comment. "That does it," he told his companion. "Still want to go?"

"If you do—and you can't do it alone." No man could take on the valley and Wass and his men.

Hume made no comment. They had rested briefly after their return to the safari camp, and Vye had been supplied with clothing from Hume's bags, so that now he wore the uniform of the Guild. He went armed, too, with the equipment belt taken from Rovald and that other's weapons, needler and tube. At least they started on their dubious rescue mission with every aid the safari camp could muster.

It was mid-afternoon when the flitter took to the air once again, scattering the hovering globes. There was no alteration in the ranks of the blue watchers waiting—for the barrier to go down, or someone in the camp to step beyond that protection?

"They're stupid," Vye said.

"Not stupid, just geared to one set of actions," Hume returned.

"Which could mean that what sends them here can't change its orders."

"Good guess. I'd say that they were governed by something akin to our tapes. No provision made for any innovations."

"So the guiding intelligence could be long gone."

"I think it has been." Hume then changed the subject sharply.

"How did you get into service at the Starfall?"

It was hard now to think back to Nahuatl—as if the Vye Lansor who had been swamper in that den of the port town was a different person altogether. In that patch of memories into which Rynch Brodie still intruded he hunted for the proper answer.

"I couldn't hold the state jobs. And once you get the habit of eating, you don't starve willingly."

"Why not the state jobs?"

"Without premium they're all low-rung tenders' places. I tried hard enough. But to sit pressing buttons when a light flashed, hour after hour—" Vye shook his head. "They said I was too erratic and gave me the shove. One more move on and it would have been compulsive conditioning. I turned port-drift instead."

"Ever thought of trying for a loan premium?"

Vye laughed shortly. "Loan premium? That's a true fantasy if you've been job hopping. None of the companies will take a chance on a man with an in and out record. Oh, I tried...." That memory arose to the surface, clear and very chilling. Yes, he had tried to break out of the net the law and custom had put around him from the day he had been made a state child. "No—it was conditioning, or port-drift."

"And you chose port-drift?"

"I was still me—as long as I stayed away from conditioning."

"Then you became Rynch Brodie in spite of your flight."

"No—well, maybe, for a while. But I'm still Vye Lansor here."

"Yes, here. And I don't think you'll have to worry about raising a premium to get a new start. You can claim victim compensation, you know."

Vye was silent, but Hume did not let him remain so.

"When the Patrol arrives, you put in your claim. I'll back you."

"You can't."

"That's where you're mistaken," Hume told him crisply. "I've already taped a full story back at the spacer—it's on record now."

Vye frowned. The Hunter seemed determined to ask for the worst the Patrol—or the planet police back on Nahuatl—could deal out. A case of illegal conditioning was about as serious as you could get.

They shot along the diagonal of the triangle made by three points, the mountain valley, Wass' camp, and the safari headquarters, heading to the slopes up which the men must be herded if the beasts were shepherding them to the mountain valley. Vye, surveying the forest thick below, began to doubt they would ever be able to pick them up before they reached the valley gate.

Hume took a weaving course, zigzagging back and forth, while they both watched intently for a glint from one of the globes, any movement which would betray that trail. And it was on one of the upper slopes that the flitter passed over two of the blue beasts lumbering along. Neither of the creatures paid any attention to the flyer, they moved with purpose on some mission of their own.

"Maybe the tail end of the hunting pack," Hume commented.

He sent the flyer hovering over a stunted line of trees and brush. Beyond that was bare rock. But though they hung for moments, nothing moved into that open.

"Wrong scent somehow." Hume brought the flitter around. He had it on manual control now, keeping it answering to the quick changes of his will.

A longer sweep supplied the answer—a vegetation roofed slit running back into the uplands, in a way resembling the crevice through which they had originally found their way into this country. Hume brought the flyer along that. But if the men they sought were pushing their way through below they could not be sighted from the air. At last, with evening drawing in, Hume was forced to admit failure.

"Wait by the gap?" Vye asked.

"Have to now." Hume glanced about. "I'd say maybe tomorrow—mid-morning before they make it that far—*if* they are here. We'll have plenty of time."

Time for what? To make ready for a pitched battle with Wass—or with the beasts herding him? To try in the space of hours to solve the mystery of the lake?

"Do you think we could blast that thing in the lake?" Vye asked.

"We might be able to, just might. But that must be the last resort. We want that in working order for the X-Tee men to study. No, we'd better plan to hold Wass at the gate, wait for the Patrol to come in."

Less than an hour later after a soaring approach, Hume brought the flitter down with neat skill on the top of one of the cliffs which helped to form the portal of the gap. There was no difference in the scene below, save that where the two bodies of the blue beasts had lain there were now only clean and shining bones.

Darkness spread out from the lake woods like a growing stain of evil promise as the sun fell behind the peaks. Night came earlier here than in the plains.

"Watch!" Vye had been gazing down the gap; he was the first to note that movement in the cloaking bush.

Out of the cover trotted a four-footed, antlered animal he had not seen before.

"Syken deer," Hume identified. "But why in the mountains? It's a long way from its home range."

The deer did not pause, but headed directly for the gap and, as it neared, Vye saw that its brown coat was roughed with patches of white froth, while more dripped from the pale pink tongue protruding from its open jaws, and its shrunken sides heaved.

"Driven!" Hume picked up a stone, hurled it to strike the ground ahead of the deer.

The creature did not start, nor show any sign of seeing the rock fall. It trotted on at the same wearied pace, passed the portal rocks into the valley. Then it stood still, wedge-shaped head up, black horns displayed, while the nose flaps expanded, testing the air, until it bounded toward the lake, disappearing in the woods.

Though they shared watches during the night there were no other signs of life, nor did the deer reappear from the woods. With the mid-morning there was a sudden sound to warn them—a wild cry which must have come from a human throat. Hume tossed one of the needlers to Vye, took the other, and they scrambled down to the floor of the gap passage.

Wass did not lead his men, he came behind the reeling trio as if he had joined the blasts as driver. And while his men wavered, staggered, gave the appearance of nearly complete exhaustion, he still walked with a steady tread, in command of his wits, his fears, and the company.

As the first of the men blundered on, a fresh trickle of red running down his bruised face, Hume called:

"Wass!"

The Veep stopped short. He made no move to unsling the needler he carried, its barrel pointing skyward over his shoulder, but his round head with its upstanding comb of hair swung slightly from side to side.

"Stop—Wass—this is a trap!"

His three men kept on. Vye moved, for Peake leading that wavering group, stumbled, would have fallen had not the younger man advanced from the shadows to steady him.

"Vye!" Hume made his name a warning.

He had only time to glance around. Wass, his broad face impassive except for the eyes—those burning madman's eyes—was aiming a ray tube.

Broken free of his hold, Peake fell to the right, came up against Hume. As Vye went down he saw Wass dart forward at a speed he wouldn't have believed a driven man could summon. The Veep lunged, escaping the shot the

Hunter had no time to aim, rolled, and came up with the needler Vye had dropped.

Then Hume, hampered by Peake's feeble clawing, met head on the swinging barrel of that weapon. He gave a startled grunt and smashed back against the cliff, a wave of scarlet blood streaming down the side of his head.

The momentum of Wass' charge carried him on. He collided with his men, and the last thing Vye saw, was the huddle of all four of them, flailing arms and legs, spinning on through the gate into the valley with Wass' hoarse, wordless shouting, bringing echoes from the cliffs.

CHAPTER THIRTEEN

He lay against a rock, and it was quiet again, except for a small whimpering sound which hurt, joined with the eating pain in his side. Vye turned his head, smelled burned cloth and flesh. Cautiously he tried to move, bring his hand across his body to the belt at his waist. One small part of his mind was very clear—if he could get his fingers to the packet there, and the contents of that packet to his mouth, the pain would go away, and maybe he could slip back into the darkness again.

Somehow he did it, pulled the packet out of its container pouch, worked the fingers of his one usable hand until he shredded open the end of the covering. The tablets inside, spilled out. But he had three or four of them in his grasp. Laboriously he brought his hand up, mouthed them all together, chewing their bitterness, swallowing them as best he could without water.

Water—the lake! For a moment he was back in time, feeling for the water bulbs he should be carrying. Then the incautious movement of his questing fingers brought a sudden stab of raw, red agony and he moaned.

The tablets worked. But he did not slide back into unconsciousness again as the throbbing torture became something remote and untroubling. With his good arm he braced himself against the cliff, managed to sit up.

Sun flashed on the metal barrel of a needler which lay in the trampled dust between him and another figure, still very still, with a pool of blood about the head. Vye waited for a steadying breath or two, then started the infinitely long journey of several feet which separated him from Hume.

He was panting heavily when he crawled close enough to touch the Hunter. Hume's face, cheek down in the now sodden dust, was dabbled with congealing blood. As Vye turned the hunter's head, it rolled limply. The other side was a mass of blood and dust, too thick to afford Vye any idea of how serious a hurt Hume had taken. But he was still alive.

With his good hand Vye thrust his numb and useless left one into the front of his belt. Then, awkwardly he tried to tend Hume. After a close inspection he thought that the mass of blood had come from a ragged tear in the scalp above the temple and the bone beneath had escaped damage. From Hume's own first-aid pack he crushed tablets into the other's slack mouth, hoping they would dissolve if the Hunter could not swallow. Then he relaxed against the cliff to wait—for what he could not have said.

Wass' party had gone on into the valley. When Vye turned his head to look down the slope he could see nothing of them. They must have tried to push on to the lake. The flitter was at the top of the cliff, as far out of his reach now as if it were in planetary orbit. There was only the hope that a rescue party from the safari camp might come. Hume had set the directional beam on the flyer, when he had brought her down, to serve as a beacon for the Patrol, if and when Starns was lucky enough to contact a cruiser.

"Hmmm...." Hume's mouth moved, cracked the drying bloody mask on his lips and chin. His eyes blinked open and he lay staring up at the sky.

"Hume—" Vye was startled at the sound of his own voice, so thready and weak, and by the fact that he found it difficult to speak at all.

The other's head turned; now the eyes were on him and there was a spark of awareness in them.

"Wass?" The whisper was as strained as his own had been.

"In there." Vye's hand lifted from Hume's chest indicating the valley.

"Not good." Hume blinked again. "How bad?" His attention was not for his own hurt; his eyes searched Vye. And the latter glanced down at his side.

By some chance, perhaps because of his struggle with Peake, Wass' beam had not struck true, the main core of the bolt passing between his arm and his side, burning both. How deeply he could not tell, in fact he did not want to find out. It was enough that the tablets had banished the pain now.

"Seared a little," he said. "You've a bad cut on your head."

Hume frowned. "Can we make the flitter?"

Vye moved, then relaxed quickly into his former position. "Not now," he evaded, knowing that neither of them would be able to take that climb.

"Beam on?" Hume repeated Vye's thoughts of moments before. "Patrol coming?"

Yes, eventually the Patrol would come—but when? Hours—days? Time was their enemy now. He did not have to say any of that, they both knew.

"Needler—" Hume's head had turned in the other direction; now his hand pointed waveringly to the weapon in the dust.

"They won't be back," Vye stated the obvious. Those others had been caught in the trap, the odds on their return without aid were very high.

"Needler!" Hume repeated more firmly, and tried to sit up, falling back with a sharp intake of breath.

Vye edged around, stretched out his leg and scraped the toe of his boot into the loop of the carrying sling, drawing the weapon up to where he could get his hand on it. As he steadied it across his knee Hume spoke again:

"Watch for trouble!"

"They all went in," Vye protested.

But Hume's eyes had closed again. "Trouble—maybe...." His voice trailed off. Vye rested his hand on the stock of the needler.

"Hoooooo!"

That beast wail—as they had heard it in the valley! Somewhere from the wood. Vye brought the needler around, so that the sights pointed in that direction. There death might be hunting, but there was nothing he could do.

A scream, filled with all the agony of a man in torment, caught up on the echoes of that other cry. Vye sighted a wild waving of bushes. A figure, very small and far away, crawled into the open on hands and knees and then crumpled into only a shadowy blot on the moss. Again the beast's cry, and a shouting!

Vye watched a second man back out of the trees, still facing whatever pursued him. He caught the glint of sun on what must be a ray tube. Leaves crisped into a black hole, curls of smoke arose along the path of that blast.

The man kept on backing, passed the inert body of his companion, glancing now and then over his shoulder at the slope up which he was making a slow but steady way. He no longer rayed the bush, but there was the crackle of a small fire outlining the ragged hole his beam had cut.

Back two strides, three. Then he turned, made a quick dash, again facing around after he had gained some yards in the open. Vye saw now it was Wass.

Another dash and an about face. But this time to confront the enemy. There were three of them, as monstrous as those Vye and Hume had fought in the same place. And one of them was wounded, swinging a charred forepaw before it, and giving voice to a wild frenzy of roars.

Wass leveled the ray tube, centering the sights on the beast nearest to him. The man hammered at the firing button with the flat of his other hand, and almost paid for that fraction of a second of distraction with his life, for the creature made one of those lightning swift dashes that Vye had earlier so luckily escaped. The clawed forepaw tore a strip from the shoulder of Wass' tunic and left sprouting red furrows behind. But the man had thrown the useless tube into its face, was now running for the gap.

Vye held the needler braced against his knee to fire. He saw the dart quiver in the upper arm of the beast, and it halted to pull out that sliver of dangerously poisoned metal, crumpled it into a tight twist. Vye continued to fire, never sure of his aim, but seeing those slivers go home in thick legs, in outstretched forelimbs, in wide, pendulous bellies. Then there were three blue shapes lying on the slope behind the man running straight for the gap.

Wass hit the invisible barrier full force, was hurled back, to lie gasping on the turf, but already raising himself to crawl again to the gateway he saw and could not believe was barred. Vye closed his eyes. He was very tired now— tired and sleepy—maybe the pain pills were bringing the secondary form of relief. But he could hear, just beyond, the man who beat at that unseen curtain, first in anger and fear, and then just in fear, until the fear was a lonesome crying that went on and on until even that last feeble assault on the barrier failed.

"We have here the tape report of Ras Hume, Out-Hunter of the Guild."

Vye watched the officer in the black and silver of the Patrol, a black and silver modified with the small, green, eye badge of X-Tee, with level and hostile gaze.

"Then you know the story." He was going to make no additions nor explanations. Maybe Hume had cleared him. All right, that was all he would ask, to be free to go his way and forget about Jumala—and Ras Hume.

He had not seen the Hunter since they had both been loaded into the Patrol flitter in the gap. Wass had come out of the valley a witless, dazed creature, still under the mental influence of whoever, or whatever, had set that trap. As far as Vye knew the Veep had not yet recovered his full senses, he might never do so. And if Hume had not dictated that confession to damn himself before the Patrol, he might have escaped. They could suspect—but they would have had no proof.

"You continue to refuse to tape?" The officer favored him with one of the closed-jaw looks Vye had often seen on the face of authority.

"I have my rights."

"You have the right to claim victim compensation—a good compensation, Lansor."

Vye shrugged and then winced at a warning from the tender skin over ribs.

"I make no claim, and no tape," he repeated. And he intended to go on saying that as long as they asked him.

This was the second visit in two days and he was getting a little tired of it all. Perhaps he should do as prudence dictated and demand to be returned to Nahuatl. Only his odd, unexplainable desire to at least see Hume kept him from making the request they would have to honor.

"You had better reconsider." Authority resumed.

"Rights of person—" Vye almost grinned as he recited that. For the first time in his pushed-around life he could use that particular phrase and make it stick. He thought there was a sour twist to the officer's mouth, but the other still retained his impersonal tone as he spoke into the intership com:

"He refused to make a tape."

Vye waited for the other's next move. This should mark the end of their interview. But instead the officer appeared to relax the restraint of his official manner. He brought a viv-root case from an inner pocket, offered a choice of contents to Vye, who gave an instant and suspicious refusal by shake of head. The officer selected one of the small tubes, snapped off the protecto-nib, and set it between his lips for a satisfying and lengthy pull. Then the panel of the cabin door pushed open, and Vye sat up with a jerk as Ras Hume, his head banded with a skin-core covering, entered.

The officer waved his hand at Vye with the air of one turning over a problem. "You were entirely right. And he's all yours, Hume."

Vye looked from one to the other. With Hume's tape in official hands why wasn't the Hunter under restraint? Unless, because they were aboard the Patrol cruiser, the officers didn't think a closer confinement was necessary. Yet the Hunter wasn't acting the role of prisoner very well. In fact he perched on a wall-flip seat with the ease of one completely at home, accepted the viv-root Vye had refused.

"So you won't make a tape," he asked cheerfully.

"You act as if you want me to!" Vye was so completely baffled by this odd turn of action that his voice came out almost plaintively.

"Seeing as how a great deal of time and effort went into placing you in the position where you *could* give us that tape, I must admit some disappointment."

"Give *us*?" Vye echoed.

The officer removed the viv-root from between his lips. "Tell him the whole sad story, Hume."

But Vye began to guess. Life in the Starfall, or as port-drift, either sharpened the wits or deadened them. Vye's had suffered the burnishing process. "A set-up?"

"A set-up," Hume agreed. Then he glanced at the Patrol officer a little defensively. "I might as well tell the whole truth—this didn't quite begin on the right side of the law. I had my reasons for wanting to make trouble for the Kogan estate, only not because of the credits involved." He moved his plasta-flesh hand. "When I found that L-B from the Largo Drift and saw the possibilities, did a little day dreaming—I worked out this scheme. But I'm a Guild man and as it happens, I want to stay one. So I reported to one of the Masters and told him the whole story—why I hadn't taped on the records my discovery on Jumala.

"When he passed along the news of the L-B to the Patrol, he also suggested that there might be room for fraud along the way I had thought it out. That started a chain reaction. It happened that the Patrol wanted Wass. But he was too big and too slick to be caught in a case that couldn't ever be broken in a court of law. They thought that here was just the bait he might snap at, and I was the one to offer it to him. He could check on me, learn that I had excellent reason to do what I said I was doing. So I approached him with my story and he liked it. We made the plan work just the way I had outlined it. And he planted Rovald on me as a check. However, I didn't know Yactisi was a plant, also."

The Patrol officer smiled. "Insurance," he waved the viv-root, "just insurance."

"What we didn't foresee was this complicating alien trouble. You were to be collected as the castaway, brought back to the Center and then, once Wass was firmly enmeshed, the Patrol would blow the thing wide open. Now we do have Wass, with your tape we'll have him for good, subject to complete reconditioning. But we also have an X-Tee puzzle which will keep the services busy for some time. And we would like your tape."

Vye watched Hume narrowly. "Then you're an agent?"

Hume shook his head. "No, just what I said I am, an Out-Hunter who happened to come into some knowledge that will assist in straightening out a few crooked quirks in several systems. I have no love for the Kogan clan, but to help bring down a Veep of Wass' measure does aid in reinstating one's self-esteem."

"This victim compensation—I *could* claim it, even though the deal was a set-up?"

"You'll have first call on Wass' assets. He has plenty invested in legitimate enterprises, though we'll probably never locate all his hidden funds. But everything we can get open title to will be impounded. Have something to do with your share?" inquired the officer.

"Yes."

Hume was smiling subtly. He was a different man from the one Vye had known on Jumala. "Premium for the Guild is one thousand credits down, two thousand for training and say another for about the best field outfit you can buy. That'll give you maybe another two or three thousand to save for your honorable retirement."

"How did you know?" Vye began and then had to laugh in spite of himself as Hume replied:

"I didn't. Good guess, eh? Well, zoom out your recorder, Commander. I think you are going to have some very free speech now." He got to his feet. "You know, the Guild has a stake in this alien discovery. We may just find that we haven't seen the last of that valley after all, recruit."

He was gone and Vye, eager to have the past done with, and the future beginning, reached for the dictation mike.

THE END

If you've enjoyed this book, you will not want to miss these terrific titles…

ARMCHAIR SCI-FI & HORROR DOUBLE NOVELS, $12.95 each

D-11 **PERIL OF THE STARMEN** by Kris Neville
THE FORGOTTEN PLANET by Murray Leinster

D-12 **THE STAR LORD** by Boyd Ellanby
CAPTIVES OF THE FLAME by Samuel R. Delany

D-13 **MEN OF THE MORNING STAR** by Edmond Hamilton
PLANET FOR PLUNDER by Hal Clement and Sam Merwin, Jr.

D-14 **ICE CITY OF THE GORGON** by Chester S. Geier and Richard Shaver
WHEN THE WORLD TOTTERED by Lester del Rey

D-15 **WORLDS WITHOUT END** by Clifford D. Simak
THE LAVENDER VINE OF DEATH by Don Wilcox

D-16 **SHADOW ON THE MOON** by Joe Gibson
ARMAGEDDON EARTH by Geoff St. Reynard

D-17 **THE GIRL WHO LOVED DEATH** by Paul W. Fairman
SLAVE PLANET by Laurence M. Janifer

D-18 **SECOND CHANCE** by J. F. Bone
MISSION TO A DISTANT STAR by Frank Belknap Long

D-19 **THE SYNDIC** by C. M. Kornbluth
FLIGHT TO FOREVER by Poul Anderson

D-20 **SOMEWHERE I'LL FIND YOU** by Milton Lesser
THE TIME ARMADA by Fox B. Holden

ARMCHAIR SCIENCE FICTION CLASSICS, $12.95 each

C-4 **CORPUS EARTHLING**
by Louis Charbonneau

C-5 **THE TIME DISSOLVER**
by Jerry Sohl

C-6 **WEST OF THE SUN**
by Edgar Pangborn

ARMCHAIR SCI-FI & HORROR GEMS SERIES, $12.95 each

G-1 **SCIENCE FICTION GEMS, Vol. One**
Isaac Asimov and others

G-2 **HORROR GEMS, Vol. One**
Carl Jacobi and others

www.ingramcontent.com/pod-product-compliance
Lightning Source LLC
Chambersburg PA
CBHW030309180626
46810CB00003B/989